"I think you could do anything you set your heart to, Maisey."

She felt herself beam. She'd heard people say that kind of thing before, but it had always sounded like a platitude. Coming from Rex, she believed it.

"And we already know you're a great mom," he continued.

She was so touched she almost gasped. Instead, she wrapped her arms around him and kissed him, full on the lips.

He leaned in and kissed her back. On the lips. Warm and strong and lingering long enough to let her know this was not a mistletoe kiss with kids watching. This was the real thing.

"I'm not supposed to kiss you," he said. "I'm very attracted to you. On so many levels. But I am leaving the day after Christmas. That's set in stone."

"Is it?" she asked before she could stop herself. Maybe if he said yes, it was, she'd stop the back-and-forth on the subject of letting herself explore her feelings for him.

"Yes. I live on the road. My job is across the entire country. That's who I am, who I've always been."

"Life changes. Things happen. We both know that. Paths twist and turn. Who says you have to stay on the same one?"

* * *

DAWSON FAMILY RANCH:
Life, love, legacy in Wyoming

Dear Reader,

One cold December day in Wyoming, US marshal Rex Dawson finds two unexpected treasures on a desolate riverbank: an adorable stray dog who needs a home and an old-fashioned bottle with a message inside. It's a letter to Santa, dated fifteen years ago, from an eight-year-old foster child who wants a parent, a family, with all her heart. Zeke has to know what happened to Maisey Clark and sets out to find her.

A single mom of a six-month-old baby, Maisey is a lot closer than Rex ever realized. With a two-week holiday vacation at the Dawson Family Guest Ranch, the guarded marshal realizes that mother and child—and that sweet stray dog—are becoming very important to him. But Rex's life is on the road—or can he learn to trust his heart?

I hope you enjoy Rex and Maisey's story. Feel free to write me with any comments or questions at MelissaSenate@yahoo.com and visit my website, melissasenate.com, for more info about me and my books. For lots of photos of my cat and dog, friend me over on Facebook, www.Facebook.com/melissasenate.

Happy holidays and happy reading!

Melissa Senate

The Long-Awaited Christmas Wish

MELISSA SENATE

HARLEQUIN

SPECIAL
EDITION

SPECIAL EDITION™

Recycling programs
for this product may
not exist in your area.

ISBN-13: 978-1-335-89490-8

The Long-Awaited Christmas Wish

Copyright © 2020 by Melissa Senate

Harlequin Enterprises ULC
22 Adelaide St. West, 40th Floor
Toronto, Ontario M5H 4E3, Canada
www.Harlequin.com

Printed in U.S.A.

Melissa Senate has written many novels for Harlequin and other publishers, including her debut, *See Jane Date*, which was made into a TV movie. She also wrote seven books for Harlequin Special Edition under the pen name Meg Maxwell. Her novels have been published in over twenty-five countries. Melissa lives on the coast of Maine with her teenage son; their rescue shepherd mix, Flash; and a lap cat named Cleo. For more information, please visit her website, melissasenate.com.

Prologue

One month ago, November

US marshal Rex Dawson thought he was alone on the footbridge across the Bear Ridge River in a rural Wyoming nature preserve, but a cute dog had come out of nowhere. The medium-size mutt was sniffing at the water's edge on the side of the bridge, just a few feet from where Rex stood. He glanced around the wilderness on all sides for the dog's owner, but he didn't see or hear anyone. Rex would know if there was anyone nearby; it was his job to be attuned to his surroundings. And because he'd been waiting over an hour for a rogue witness who hadn't shown up, Rex had been on red alert.

"Hey, buddy, you alone out here?" Rex asked, walking over to where the stray was pawing at something in the water against the wooden post of the bridge.

The dog looked up at him, head tilted. Some kind of shepherd mix, Rex figured, taking in the cinnamon and black markings and the tall, pointy ears that had to be four inches high. Rex glanced at what had caught the dog's interest. A bottle—with what looked like a rolled-up piece of paper inside. It was one of those old-fashioned glass milk jugs, the kind with a wide neck and body and a metal cap.

"Message in a bottle?" Rex asked the dog, giving him a pat behind his ears.

He picked up the dirty bottle. He knew this type well. Rex had grown up on a dude ranch that his grandparents had started, and the family's milk had come from their cow, Lizzie. His grandmother had liked old-fashioned milk bottles, but with the hinged tops. When his grandparents had passed on fourteen years ago and his dad had inherited the Dawson Family Guest Ranch, Bo Dawson had soon sold off the animals to pay for his drinking and gambling addictions and there was rarely milk in the fridge, despite his six kids. "Water is free and comes right out of the tap," Bo would say, pointing at the sink. Rex still couldn't think of the ranch without his dad coming to mind.

"Some things never change, buddy," he told the dog. The sweet-faced mutt stared at Rex with those old-soul amber eyes. No collar. Too skinny. Dirty. A little on the timid side. He looked cold and lonely and hungry. Definitely a stray. "C'mon," Rex said. "Let's go warm up in my truck and we'll see what the note in the bottle says."

The dog tilted his head again and seemed to be saying, *You talking to me?* Rex headed for the small gravel parking lot, his new friend following. He got a blanket from the cargo area of his SUV and made a bed of sorts on the passenger seat. "Up you go," Rex said, and the dog hopped in. Rex turned on the ignition, heat filling the vehicle, and the dog sighed and stretched out his long, narrow snout, resting his chin on Rex's knee.

Aww. He petted his new buddy behind the ears, then looked at the bottle. "So let's see what this message says." He uncapped the bottle and fished out the rolled-up yellowed paper. It was a letter to Santa, dated fifteen years ago.

Dear Santa,
All I want for Christmas is a family. Just a mom OR a dad would be fine. I'm not

picky. I would also really love to have a brother or a sister. But if that's asking for too much, I'll just take a mom or dad. I've been really good this year. You can ask Miss Meredith—she runs the foster home.
Maisey Clark, eight years old
Prairie City, Wyoming

One-two punch straight to the heart. Damn. He could just picture little Maisey Clark, sitting in her foster home in Prairie City and writing out this note in her best handwriting. He imagined her swiping an empty milk bottle, sliding in the rolled-up letter to Santa and tossing it out into the river, hoping it carried all the way to the north pole.

The bottle certainly hadn't gotten very far. "But I hope her Christmas wish came true," he said to the dog. "Think it did, River?"

River. Guess he'd named the stray. For where he'd found him, where he'd found the bottle, containing a fifteen-year-old letter to Santa.

He had to know. Actually, it was more than that—he *needed* to know that Maisey Clark had gotten her family. Between the cold, skinny stray dog and the fervent wish for a parent, Rex knew he should be counting his blessings. Yeah, his job was stressful and he'd been through some stuff he'd like to forget. But he had family. Despite losing his dad last December when the two of them had unfinished business, the six Dawson siblings were always there for one another. Sometimes he didn't appreciate that enough.

"What do you think happened to Maisey, River?" he asked. "She'd be twenty-three now." He really hoped her wish had come true. That she'd been adopted by a wonderful family. "Maybe they even had a cute pooch like you."

River licked his hand and looked at him with those sweet eyes.

"I sure would like to take you home," he said, petting River's side. "But I don't really have one. I have a condo in Cheyenne I rarely use because I'm always on the road."

Right now, he was hours from that condo but just outside Bear Ridge, where he'd grown up and spent as little time as possible. He couldn't rescue a dog when he was home maybe once every three months and otherwise lived in hotels across the country.

"I do know where to take you, though," he said, scratching River under the chin. "The Dawson Family Guest Ranch. My sister and two of my brothers live on the property, and if one of them can't take you in, they'll find you a good home." He had no doubt about that.

Rex pulled out of the parking lot, his head a jumble of Christmas wishes, stray dogs, rogue witnesses and tomorrow's three meetings, including escorting a witness to court. Day after tomorrow he'd be accompanying a seventy-two-year-old widower to his new life in the Florida Keys, going over protocol of the witness protection program and sticking around for a while to get him acclimated to life under a new identity. Rex knew that wasn't easy. But being on the run, scared and alone, wasn't easy, either. Rex hoped to find his missing witness—the one who'd agreed to meet him at the river today but hadn't—by Christmas.

Finding Maisey Clark should be a lot easier. If not a simple Google search, then through his access to databases. He had to know what happened, that Maisey *had* gotten a family. He wasn't one to believe in Christmas wishes—or any kind—coming true. But for Maisey he'd make an exception.

Chapter One

Two weeks before Christmas

Rex was one for three on his must-do list. Finding Maisey Clark not only *hadn't* been easy, but impossible. He'd tried everything, but her name never came up in any of his searches. He took it to mean she'd been adopted and therefore had a different last name. He wanted to believe that, anyway. He had managed to get in touch with the "Miss Meredith" who Maisey had mentioned in her letter, but the foster mother had told him Maisey had moved to a different group foster home the following year, and given her age, Meredith doubted she'd been adopted, though she'd been unable to say for sure. Not knowing made him itchy.

And his rogue witness never responded to any of Rex's calls or texts. Not that Rex was giving up on him. The past few days Rex had been chasing down leads in Montana, determined to find the guy. Rex believed in justice—for the victim and family, for the witness's future, for the criminal to rot in prison. Rex was running on fumes, but he hadn't agreed with his boss that he needed two weeks off leading to Christmas. The boss had insisted. And so here Rex was, with two weeks R & R on the Dawson Family Guest Ranch. He'd still work during his time off. He had to.

The one thing Rex had accomplished? Getting that sweet stray dog a new home—right here at the ranch with his sister, Daisy, who'd fallen for River on sight. Despite being a busy new mother of a five-month-old baby and the guest relations manager of the ranch, she'd adored River so much that she'd hoped no one would claim him. River hadn't had a microchip, and after checking with local shelters and posting ads, no one had come for the dog. River was hers.

Now Rex sat in Daisy's big country kitchen in the farmhouse he grew up in. River was asleep in his plush blue dog bed by the stone fireplace.

When he'd arrived at Daisy's this morning, officially on vacation, he'd gotten a serious welcome from the pooch he'd rescued from that cold riverside, the dog so excited to see him that Rex vowed to come visit more often. His family and River. He'd only been at the ranch for a few hours, catching up with his siblings who lived and worked on the ranch, but coming home early for Christmas might have been a good idea after all. He did need this break. He had some things to figure out—and he wasn't even sure what those things were. That he felt unsettled was an understatement.

All he knew was that ever since his brother Noah had rebuilt the guest ranch last spring, the place *didn't* remind him of home—a word that had always come with baggage. He liked the ranch now, could breathe here, think here.

"I have a very attractive, interesting woman in mind for you," Daisy said, setting out ham, cheese, a delicious-looking baguette and mayo and mustard on the kitchen table.

River opened an eye, smelling lunch.

Rex cut the bread. Daisy was a notorious matchmaker. "Let me stop you right there. I'm here for two weeks, then back on the road."

Daisy narrowed her eyes at him. "Are you ever going to tell us what you do? Noah thinks you're a spy. I say FBI."

Rex smiled. He'd never told his family what his job was because of the nature of the work; it had to remain secret and so he chose not to discuss it. "I'll tell you this—you're on the right track. But trust me, my job is the main reason you shouldn't fix me up, Daisy. How can I have a relationship when I'm never home? I don't even have a home, not really."

"This *is* home, Rex. Forget that sterile one-bedroom condo in Cheyenne. Build a luxe cabin like Axel did on the property. We have thousands of acres in the Wyoming wilderness. You can still do whatever it is you do with the ranch as your base."

She wasn't wrong about that. But he'd spent so much time thinking of this ranch as *not* home that building a cabin on the property hadn't really entered his mind, no matter how much he liked the place now. He was planning to stay with Axel the first week of his vacation and Daisy the second. Their brother Noah and his wife, Sara, lived in the foreman's cabin just a quarter mile down the road with their twins and there wasn't room for Rex, though they'd invited him anyway, because they were nice that way. "Our sofa is your sofa," Noah had said.

With Daisy's baby, Noah's eight-month-old twins and Axel's toddler, there were already quite a few members of the next generation of Dawsons. And they were far removed from the not-so-great last fifteen years. Those little ones would grow up entirely differently than their parents had, with a real appreciation of the Dawson Family Guest Ranch and its history.

"Wait," Daisy said. "Did I just hear Tony?" She cocked an ear toward the stairs and the nursery on the second floor. Pure silence. "Nope. Or maybe he fussed and soothed himself back to sleep. Harrison and I have been working on that."

Rex had gotten to see his cute nephew for about ten minutes this morning before the tyke had yawned so hard Daisy had had to put him down for a nap.

Daisy sat, and they made their sandwiches. "Hey, guess what," she said. "We're restarting an old Dawson Family Guest Ranch annual tradition—a daylong Christmas fair like Gram and Gramps used to put on for the guests. Remember?"

He remembered. He'd loved those fairs, which always included reindeer and a Santa hut, multicolored lights everywhere. His grandparents had always seemed magical to him, despite how homespun and rooted and practical they were.

"We always have a lot of kids, but with the Christmas fair advertising, bookings with children skyrocketed, so I hired a full-time nanny for our babysitting program." Daisy told him all about the Kid Zone, a huge room in the lodge staffed by a few energetic employees so that guests could drop off their children to partake in ranch activities the kids might be too young for or not interested in. "The nanny oversees the Kid Zone and the three sitters. I'm telling ya, Maisey Clark is a godsend. She's been here only a couple days and—"

Rex almost dropped his ham-and-cheese sandwich. "Wait, Daisy. Did you say *Maisey Clark*?"

"Yes. Why? You know her?"

He stared at Daisy, barely able to believe this. "Is she in her early twenties?"

"She's twenty-three, but has a lot of childcare experience and great references. Why?"

Eight plus fifteen. Bingo. He'd been trying to track down this woman for a month and here she was? Mind-boggling. "I think I do know her. Sort of. I'll tell you about it after I confirm it's the same Maisey Clark."

"The Kid Zone closes at six. First floor in the lodge. Big colorful sign at the end of the hall."

River came padding over and put his furry black chin on Rex's thigh. *We found her, River,* he silently told his buddy while petting his head. *Now we'll learn if her Christmas wish came true.*

He sure hoped it had. Because he felt like something deep inside would settle, that wrongs would be righted, that foster kids writing to Santa for a mom or a dad would be heard.

He wanted to rush over to the lodge right now, but he figured he'd wait till closing time, when she wasn't busy and surrounded by children. Maisey Clark was a half mile away from where he sat. The coincidence *had* to mean something. *What* he didn't know, but it was Christmastime and it seemed like close to a miracle.

Maisey Clark added a stuffed reindeer, two small balls and three action figures to the big basket she carried around the various sections of the Kid Zone. She looked around the colorful space, each area marked for different age groups. Spotless. Her second workday at the Dawson Family Guest Ranch's childcare center was over, all the kids—and the huge room in the lodge—picked up.

She closed her eyes for a second, barely able to believe she'd gotten this perfect-for-her job just when she'd hit rock bottom last week. Her previous full-time job at a day care barely paid enough for Maisey, a single mother without support from anywhere, to make rent and utilities, let alone keep her six-month-old daughter in diapers. But there'd been cutbacks and Maisey had been let go and she'd been frantic.

The posting she'd noticed for this job—nanny at the Dawson Family Guest Ranch—was so perfect she hadn't dared hope to get it, but she had. Room, board and a salary—plus Maisey could bring her baby to work. "Room" was a small but cute and clean cabin nestled in the woods just a quarter mile from the lodge. "Board" was free meals and snacks in the ranch's amazing cafeteria. Omelets for breakfast. All the soup and salad and sandwiches she could eat at lunch. And entrées for dinner she hadn't been able to afford in the grocery store, like fish and steak. The salary wouldn't come for another week when she received her first paycheck, but she had enough diapers and baby food to get her through. She was used to buying secondhand for her baby girl when it came to pajamas and her snowsuit and just about everything in her tiny nursery in the cabin, but it was Christmastime, and Maisey would love to buy Chloe something special. She'd see.

If there was one thing Maisey understood, it was that the rug could be yanked when you least expected it. Oh, she thought her husband loved her? Nope. Would care that he had a child coming into the world? Nope. Long gone. Never met Chloe and wasn't interested. Nor was his family, since he'd told them Chloe wasn't even *his*—liar. A job that seemed secure? Ha. No such thing. Maisey Clark was a realist. The most important thing was building a nest egg, an emergency stash of cash in the bank for when the rug did get pulled. A friend and coworker from the day care had told Maisey to find herself a sugar daddy to marry, but first of all: *ew*, and second of all: no. Maisey would stand on her own two feet. She could only rely on herself, something she was well used to.

She took the basket over to the check-in desk; housekeeping would pick up all the toys for disinfecting from sticky little fingers coated with animal cracker crumbs and juice box drippings. She loved those sticky fingers. Maisey adored the children, from infants to teenagers, who'd come through the Kid Zone the past two days. Not that she hadn't gotten peed on by a baby—once (a rookie mistake)—and broken up two bad arguments and had to call one boy's parents to pick him up because he wouldn't follow the rules. She took the bad with the good. Working with children, listening to them, being there for them, had been all she'd ever wanted to do. Her heart had been set on being a teacher, but affording college was still a pipe dream. One day, she'd get there.

For now, all she wanted was to go home to

her sweet little cabin, heat up last night's left-over pasta carbonara from the ranch cafeteria and watch a funny movie. Maybe some mindless reality TV.

She heard the door to the Kid Zone open with its loud jangle and she turned around. A man came in, glancing around, his eyes stopping on her. His entire body stopped, too. He just stood there staring at her with a look on his face she couldn't read.

"Maisey Clark?"

Uh-oh, she thought, taking in the tall, dark-haired guy with the assessing blue eyes and wondering what he could possibly want with her. It wasn't so much that he looked like a cop that he seemed like one. He worked in some official capacity—that much she was sure of. The way he'd said her name. The way he was staring at her as if sizing her up. She walked over to him holding the basket against her stomach like a shield. "Yes, I'm Maisey Clark. What can I do for you?"

"I have something that I think belongs to you," he said, reaching into the backpack on his shoulder and pulling out something covered in Bubble Wrap.

What could it be? Did she even own anything breakable? With a six-month-old baby and a job taking care of many kids big and small all day, she wasn't the Bubble Wrap type.

As he unwrapped it, she gasped, her hand covering her mouth. "Omigosh," she whispered.

It was a bottle. A dirty, scratched-up old milk bottle with a metal cap. And there was a rolled-up piece of paper inside. She knew what that note said. She knew because she wrote it. Fifteen years ago.

"You found this?" She shook her head. "I can't believe it."

"What I can't believe is that you're right here, working at my family's ranch, when I've been looking for you for a month. I'm Rex Dawson," he added, shifting the bottle to his left hand and extending his right one.

She shook his hand, warm and strong. "Mais—" she began, then smiled. "Well, you know who I am. "*And* what I wanted for Christmas when I was eight years old." Suddenly that seemed a little too personal, like he knew too much about her. "Where'd you find it?"

"About ten minutes from here by a footbridge across the Bear Ridge River." He held it out to her.

"Well, that's no surprise," she said, taking the bottle and sighing. Part of her wanted to pull out the note and read it, but another part couldn't bear to. "That it didn't get very far. On its route to the north pole," she added with a smile.

"That must mean what you wrote, what you wished for, never came true." He looked kind of crestfallen, which touched her.

"Nope. Never did." As she was hit with a few memories she didn't want to think about, she changed the subject. "You're a cop, right? Or work for the state in some capacity?"

His eyes widened. He seemed both surprised and impressed. "Federal law enforcement. But how could you know that? My own family doesn't know what I do for a living."

"When you're a foster kid, you get used to officials—how they sound, how they stand, the way they look you over, assessing. So you're FBI?"

"US marshal," he said.

"I was close."

He laughed, but then sobered. "Alarmingly so. I'm not sure why I was so forthcoming. My family doesn't even know what my job is exactly."

"Well, you know my biggest secret—what I used to want for Christmas more than anything, and now I know yours."

He gave her something of a smile and seemed to be assessing again.

"When you first said my name, I thought maybe

you were a dad here to pick up your child and didn't realize your wife beat you to it. No kids left," she added, waving an arm at the empty room.

He glanced around the huge space, which had several well-marked sections—for babies and toddlers, for preschoolers, for big kids and for teens. There were play structures, a rock wall, basketball hoops, a library, chairs and tables, countless beanbags, games, lots of balls and foam blocks and the Kid Zone sitters besides herself to watch the kids like a hawk. Maisey always took care of the babies and toddlers. Because the six cabins at the Dawson Family Guest Ranch were booked from two-day packages to weeks at a time, the guests were always changing.

He raised an eyebrow. "Well, that would be impossible since I'm not married and don't have kids and don't plan to."

She felt her smile fade. Something in the way he'd said that told her he meant it, that something had happened. Bad experience, maybe. She knew all about that.

"And there *is* one left," he said. "That quiet little baby over there." He pointed behind her.

She turned and smiled at the sleeping baby girl. "That's actually my daughter, Chloe. She's six months old. Perk of the job is getting to bring her to work."

He looked at the baby, then back at her. "At first I thought the reason I couldn't find you in the system was because you'd been adopted and your last name changed. Then just a minute ago, I figured you'd gotten married. But if you did, you clearly kept your maiden name, so now I'm confused why I couldn't find you."

"I got married at eighteen and was so excited to join my husband's family, take his name. But turns out he wasn't very family-oriented. Or vows-oriented. I tried to make things work, and when I finally got pregnant, he told me we were through. I haven't seen him since that night."

Oh, Lordy. Why had she said all that? She could feel her cheeks burning and turned slightly away from him.

"So you took back your maiden name," he said gently.

She nodded. "Very recently. I missed the connection to my parents, anyway. They didn't leave me on purpose. I'm glad to be Maisey Clark again. And I do have a family now—with Chloe and our cat, Snowbell. So really, I did get a family—just took fifteen years from the time I wrote that letter."

The look on Rex Dawson's face, pure compassion, had her off balance. *Thanks but no thanks.* Anytime she got personal, talked about her past, which was rare for her, she felt so vulnerable, so exposed. She hated the "oh, you poor thing" pity she got whenever she was put in a position to mention how she'd grown up.

Chloe's eyes fluttered open, and Maisey walked over to the baby swing and lifted her up.

"Guess I'd better get this little one home," she said, kneeling in front of her open tote bag for Chloe's fleece snowsuit. "I live in the cabin between here and the cafeteria." She pulled out the snowsuit, the bag still overstuffed with everything she and a baby could need for an eight-hour day in the Kid Zone, from extra onesies to two changes of clothes for Maisey in case she was thrown up on—it had happened twice her first day—to bottles and diapers. She tried to get the milk bottle inside, but there wasn't room, so she started taking things out to reconfigure.

"I'll walk you home and carry the bottle for you," he said. "It's my fault you have an extra thing to lug."

"I've got it," Maisey said, but now a burp cloth had gotten stuck in the zipper in her haste to get going. "Or not," she added with a sigh.

Accept help when you need it. Rule of getting by in life, she reminded herself.

He extended his hand for the bottle. She smiled and gave it to him, extricating the burp cloth and managing to shove everything back in and get the bag zipped up this time.

"You know, I'm glad you found it and brought it to me," she said, standing up. "I have closure on it now. One of my foster sisters and I wrote letters to Santa that same day and we both threw our bottles in the creek that ran behind the home. She was a year older than I was and said she didn't believe in Santa, but since I did, I would get what I wanted and she surely wouldn't. Two days later, an estranged aunt came to take her home and formally adopted her by that Christmas. She called to tell me she'd believe in Santa even when she was ninety-nine."

Maisey smiled at the memory of her sweet friend with the long auburn hair and freckles.

"Are you two still in touch?" he asked, putting the bottle in his backpack and slinging it over his shoulder. Broad, she couldn't help but notice.

"We lost touch when I got moved out of Miss Meredith's group home. But I'm glad she got all my Christmas spirit. I never was able to get it back," she said, then rolled her eyes at herself for saying too much again.

Even though she wasn't looking at him—she was looking anywhere but at him—she could tell he was studying her.

"Well, I have a quarter of Christmas spirit,

maybe an eighth, so I get it," he said. "I'm hoping I get to half by the big day."

She stared at him. "Why? You have a burning
Christmas wish?"

"More like there are some things I want to
accomplish—work related. And some things I
need to figure out."

"Well, the ranch is definitely the place for that,"
she said. "I'm from Prairie City, which is still
plenty quiet despite it being a bigger town, but
out here in the wilderness, you can really think."

"That's what I'm hoping for." He unexpectedly picked up her big pink tote and put it on his
other shoulder.

Good-looking *and* kind.

She got Chloe bundled in her fleece snowsuit
with the bear ears, the much-appreciated gift from
her former coworkers at the day care. Once Chloe
was settled into her stroller, they went into the
hallway of the grand lodge. She locked up and
turned the sign on the door over, indicating the
Kid Zone was closed till 9:00 a.m. tomorrow.

"Christmas is everywhere on the ranch," she
said, eyeing the huge tree, trimmed to the nines,
by the curving staircase at the end of the hall.
"Honestly, sometimes it's hard to look at, and
sometimes a piece of red tinsel will remind me

of my parents and I want to wrap myself in it, you know?"

Ugh. There was that compassion on his face again. Why was she being so talkative, so open with this guy? She didn't know him at all.

The bottle, the memory—of everything it invoked—had done a number on her, most likely. Maisey always like to think she was immune to nostalgia and sentiment. And then whammo. Her mother's voice. Her dad's hugs. She'd have to close her eyes, wanting to keep them close and push them away at the same time.

Story of her life.

"Honestly, it's hard for me to just be on this property," he said, his gaze on the tree. "Unfinished business. Christmas always makes me feel pressured to come here, to count my blessings, to slow down. I want to be here *and* on a plane flying away right now."

"So you get it," she said, goose bumps on the nape of her neck. He *really* got it. "But I *am* counting my blessings. I have my Chloe. And I have this job. I was getting really worried about my bank account when I saw the ad posted for the nanny job at the ranch."

"I'm glad it worked out," he said on almost a whisper, and she glanced at him, wondering what he was thinking. She didn't see pity in his expression. Then again, it was his job to have a poker face.

His gaze moved to Chloe. "Your baby looks very content. My three siblings who live on the ranch all have kids—babies and a toddler, so I'm learning to read faces and cries for when I need to babysit."

She smiled. "Uncle Rex."

"Another thing I never thought I'd be. Now I have three nephews and a niece. Proving that old adage right—life is full of surprises."

"Good and bad," she said, then immediately wished she could take it back. *Stop telling him your every thought*, she silently yelled at herself.

"I'd clink to that if I were holding a glass of eggnog."

She laughed. "I *love* eggnog. I might not have any Christmas spirit, but I never pass up eggnog."

Once outside in the cold, biting air, she stared at the two evergreens flanking the lodge, both festooned with white lights. Beautiful—but she tried to avoid looking at them.

"When Chloe's a little older—two, I guess— I'll get more into Christmas, I'm sure," she said. "The last thing she needs is Mom saying *bah humbug*. Christmas is everything to kids."

He glanced at her, and she could tell he was thinking about the eight-year-old whose Christmas wish hadn't come true. *Darn it. Shut up, Maisey. Stop. Talking.*

They headed down the gravel path that led to her cabin. It was nestled in the woods, and she loved it. Her boss, Daisy, Rex's sister, had hung a beautiful wreath on the door as a welcome gift, and Maisey had been so touched. It was the perfect amount of Christmas. Enough to serve as a reminder but not enough to make her go into the bathroom and sob.

At the cabin, she unlocked the door and wheeled in the stroller, Rex right behind her with the tote bag. He put it down, then unzipped his backpack and pulled out the bottle, which he set on the console table. Right beside a photo of her and her parents, a Christmas tree behind them. Maisey had been five. But by Christmas Eve she'd been in the foster home that Miss Meredith ran.

He picked up the photo. "I can understand why Christmas is hard for you." He put the frame down.

She felt tears stinging. "This is Chloe's first Christmas, though. I hate being a Scrooge. It's not fair to her. I should at least get a tree for the cabin."

"I can picture one right by the window," he said, looking in that direction, then all around the sparsely decorated open-concept first floor. She only had the basics for furniture since she and her ex had lived in a trailer with a lot of built-ins.

Once she got her first paycheck, she'd see what she truly needed.

"There's a great Christmas tree farm in Bear Ridge about five minutes from here," he said. "It's open till ten and well lit. I'd be happy to take you tomorrow night. My treat. As a welcome gift."

She looked down at Chloe in the stroller, her hazel eyes so alert. *New traditions*, she told herself. *For Chloe. Do it for her.* "You Dawsons sure are nice," she said. "Your sister gave me the wreath on the door." She wouldn't be able to afford a tree otherwise, not for a week, anyway, so although she didn't love taking what felt like charity, she nodded. "Thank you."

And just like that, he was picking her up from the lodge at six tomorrow. With a peekaboo to Chloe and a smile to her, he left. The minute the door closed behind him, she felt his absence.

"What's up with that, Snowbell?" she asked as her white cat padded over to slink between her ankles. She knelt down to scratch Snowbell by her tail, her favorite spot. "Good-looking. Kind. Knows too much about me."

Maisey Clark had been stomped on by the giant boot of heartache, and picking herself up from that—from her parents' deaths, to the constant disappointment of never getting adopted, to her husband's betrayal—had been tough. That last one she'd gotten through because of Chloe. Her daughter needed her.

She took Chloe out of her stroller, peeling her from the bear fleece snowsuit, relishing the soft weight of her baby in her arms. She snuggled Chloe against her chest. She had everything she needed now. And tomorrow night she'd have a tree, too—for her daughter.

What she didn't need? A hot, generous man distracting her from what was important. She'd thank Rex Dawson for his thoughtfulness when they lugged the tree here, and that would be that. No talking, no sharing, no gut-spilling. No imagining herself in that gorgeous man's arms. Fantasies like that were all too easy to make come true. But cold hard reality always came around—the next morning or a few weeks or even a few years later.

If she was actually going to have a little Christmas for her daughter, the last thing Maisey wanted was to ruin it.

Chapter Two

The next afternoon, as Rex helped his two-year-old nephew, Danny, build a tower of blocks in his brother Axel's mansion-like log cabin, he couldn't stop thinking about Maisey. That she was *real*—the person behind the letter to Santa. That she was so pretty with big pale brown eyes, long silky blond hair in a ponytail down her back. His reaction to her had caught him by surprise. Of course, he knew there would be a connection because of the bottle, the letter inside, but everything about her—particularly her honesty or maybe her vulnerability—drew him hard. She was so young, just twenty-three. She deserved the anticipation of a bright, shiny future. Instead, she could barely stomach Christmas.

Not that Rex should talk. At thirty-one, he was as world-weary and cynical as they came, having seen the worst of people and what the worst could do to law-abiding citizens. Rex had been a marshal for so long that distancing himself from people was ingrained.

That he wanted to kiss Maisey goodbye last night, even on the cheek, though he'd been thinking about her lips, wasn't a good sign. It meant he was both emotionally and physically attracted. He was leaving in less than two weeks, the day after Christmas, and he had no doubt in his mind that Maisey Clark needed a forever kind of man, someone ready to settle down and be the great husband she deserved, the great father to her baby daughter. He wasn't that guy. So he'd better forget about her lips and face and hair and how powerfully drawn to her he was. Maybe it was a protective thing.

Yes. That was it. That made sense. She was young with so much responsibility, and she'd had no one behind her since she was a very young child. He felt protective; of course he did.

Though if Maisey barely wanted a Christmas tree, he had no doubt she didn't want a relationship mucking up the works, either. Which also made him feel oddly protective of her. He *wanted* her to want, to hope, to dream.

"Unck Rex, higher!" Danny said, pointing at the top of their tower, which was about three feet and just a little taller than his nephew.

"Higher? I'd better put you on my shoulders so you can get the blocks up there," Rex said, and the little blond imp climbed on, a block in each hand. Rex was on his knees and Danny added the blocks, cheering and pumping his little fist in the air.

"You are so meant to be a dad."

Startled by the voice and the comment, Rex turned—carefully since he had a toddler on his shoulders—to find his sister-in-law Sadie smiling at him, his brother Axel behind her as they came in the front door. And behind them were the dogs—Axel's yellow Lab, Dude, and River. Last night, when Rex had been leaving Daisy's to go to the lodge with the bottle, River had followed him out and lain down in front of his path, putting his chin on Rex's shoe. Daisy had said River was clearly trying to tell them something—that he knew he was meant to be with Rex. He reminded his sister that he lived on the road and in crummy hotels and couldn't take on a dog, and Daisy had said she'd consider herself River's foster mother until Rex figured out that he belonged on the ranch.

You had to hand it to Daisy for trying.

So now River would be staying with him at Axel and Sadie's, which they were more than fine with. River had such a sweet temperament and was gentle with Danny, who was well used to dogs since he lived with Dude. And the two pooches had become best buds.

And if Rex were honest, he'd admit how much he liked having River with him. The dog had felt like his from the moment he'd rescued him. That feeling, though, the *belonging*, grated on him, and he wasn't sure why.

But that discomfort was always with him, and it was why he *wasn't* meant to be a dad. Luckily, there was so much noise and activity right now that Rex didn't have to comment on what Sadie had said.

Axel and Sadie took off their zillion layers— hats, gloves, scarves, boots—then came into the living room. Rex set his nephew down and he went leaping into his dad's arms, who hoisted him high and turned him upside down and sideways to his son's complete joy.

"Oh, God, Axel, don't make him throw up lunch—and all over my favorite rug," Sadie said, laughing.

Axel grinned and gave Danny a big kiss on the cheek and set his son down.

"Can I knock over the blocks, Unck Rex?" Danny asked.

"That is what they're for!" Rex said with a grin. "On three. One. Two—"

Danny charged ahead, gleefully knocking the foam blocks all over his play area. He tossed two handfuls up in the air and let them rain down on him and the dogs. Dude and River gave the blocks a sniff, then went into their beds by the fireplace, River with his favorite toy in his mouth, a squeaky stuffed squirrel that Rex had bought him the day he'd brought him over to the ranch.

Okay, so he did love that dog. Fine. But when it came to relationships with *two*-legged creatures, he was better off just avoiding them altogether. He met terrific women on the road all the time, often at hotel bars across the country where he'd go to unwind after a rough day, and those times when he really needed the company in every way, he was completely honest. Those encounters always left him feeling empty, though. The last time he'd actually tried a relationship—with a fellow marshal, a woman he'd really fallen for—she'd blasted him when he couldn't propose after six months of dating, of long-distance phone calls and hard-to-arrange rendezvous. *This is the real point*, she'd said, wagging a finger between them. *Love.*

He had loved her—he was pretty sure, anyway—

but he hadn't been able to bring himself to propose. So maybe he hadn't loved her? Maybe he just wasn't ready for a lifetime commitment? *Or maybe I'm just not the right woman*, she'd thrown at him before storming out of his life. That was six months ago.

Rex sighed and stared at the beautifully decorated Christmas tree by the floor-to-ceiling windows across the room. There were countless brightly wrapped gifts around the tree, a few with his name on them, which he saw when Danny had led him over to ask him to point out the ones with *his* name.

Rex thought about what his sister said earlier, before Rex had left for the lodge to meet Maisey. *Oh, you should know—about dating? Axel said the same thing. Not interested. Look at him now. Married with a baby on the way and a very doting daddy.*

Rex could hardly believe it. Fatherhood sure did suit Axel, though. But Rex? No. Being a doting uncle was easy.

Fatherhood was something else. All the Dawson siblings knew that. Even if half of them were now—quite happily—parents.

He thought about the difference between this cabin and Maisey's—the complete lack of holiday decorations in her place, despite her wanting to give her baby girl a special first Christmas.

From what Maisey had said about her finances and from the lack of furniture in her cabin, she didn't have much.

He'd stop by the general store in town, which had lots of garland and lights and tree-topper stars and ornaments. Then after they brought home her tree tonight, he could help her trim it. Over the next week and a half he'd add lots of gifts for Maisey and her baby and even a catnip mouse or two for Snowbell. Yes. He'd give Maisey the Christmas she'd been long owed and the one her baby girl deserved, and he could drive off back to his life on the road, belonging nowhere and to no one. The way he liked it.

But his gaze landed on River, his cinnamon-and-black body curled up in the plush red plaid bed, the old-soul amber eyes soft on Rex. *We belong to each other*, the dog seemed to be saying.

Luckily, his nephew chose that moment to catapult into his lap for a giant hug and Rex stopped thinking too far ahead.

"Would you like to make an ornament with your name on it for the tree?" Maisey asked the girl sitting by herself on a mat and looking glum. "We have a whole 'make your own' station over there," Maisey said, pointing. The table, overseen by one of Maisey's very energetic staffers, had been a huge hit today.

It was five thirty and only two kids remained in the Kid Zone, nine-year-old Zara and thirteen-year-old Tyler, who had been shooting hoops for almost an hour straight and showed no signs of tiring. The dribbling and ball landing with a hard bounce had become kind of soothing ambient noise. Tyler's parents and younger sister were at the petting zoo presentation on the animals. Earlier this afternoon, the sister had been in the Kid Zone while the parents and Tyler went fly-fishing. Zara and her parents had arrived at the ranch today and were staying through Christmas.

The girl's hazel eyes were a combination of pissed off and hurt. Maisey only got to notice when Zara pushed her long dark hair away from her face.

"Nope" was the response as Zara crossed her arms over her chest and stared straight ahead.

Tough customer, Maisey thought. "Maybe a game of jacks or cards? Crazy Eights?"

"No and no." Zara wouldn't even look at Maisey.

"I think your mom said she'd be back to pick you up at 5:45. That's fifteen minutes to fill. What are you in the mood to do?"

"First of all, I know how to tell time. Second of all, nothing!" With that, Zara got up and stalked over to a purple beanbag and flopped herself down.

Yikes. Angry and disrespectful, which Maisey would let pass because it was her job to know when to discipline and when to give a kid some space. She also knew that when a kid was hurting, they usually didn't want to be left alone. But in this case, she got the sense she should give Zara a little time to cool down.

Still, that didn't mean Maisey couldn't say one more thing. She made a show of picking up errant balls and blocks and dumping them into a basket she held. There was a stuffed tiger by Zara's beanbag. She headed over and picked it up.

"Zara, I didn't mean to crowd you. Just let me know if you need or want anything."

That seemed to enrage the girl even more. She snapped her head fast in the opposite direction. What mattered right now was that Zara knew Maisey was here for her.

The door opened, and Tyler's dad came in. "Hey, buddy. Time to wash up for dinner. I hear it's burrito night at the caf."

Tyler nodded, dribbling the ball up to the hoop. "He shoots, he scores, the crowd goes—" he said as he shot the final basket. And missed.

"Mild!" Zara finished, rolling her eyes.

Tyler laughed good-naturedly and chased down the ball and shot a three-pointer. "You mean wild!

Whoooo. Whooosh," he said, making a mega-phone around his mouth.

Zara rolled her eyes again and turned away.

Maisey waved a hello at Tyler's dad and the two left. Half a minute later, Zara's parents came in. You could hear the girl's sigh clear across the room. Interesting. The bad mood extended to her folks.

"Hi, Zara!" her mom said with what looked like a cautious smile to Maisey. "I hear it's bur-rito night in the caf tonight. You get to choose your fillings."

"At least I like burritos," Zara muttered, get-ting up from the beanbag.

Maisey noticed the mom and dad give each other a look. Had Zara meant she didn't like her mom with that "at least"? The tension from the girl definitely carried over as she headed out, re-fusing her dad's hand.

Family angst. Whatever was going on, the parents seemed loving and caring. Maisey knew everything was relative and she couldn't com-pare her lack of parents to Zara's, but she couldn't help thinking, *You have no idea how lucky you are.* What she would have given for someone to care that she loved burritos. Or that when she was young and then a teenager, she missed hav-ing parents, people who loved her, cared about her, *so* badly that she'd have to go very still until she could get ahold of herself, accept the un-acceptable.

Rex Dawson was going to be here soon to take her tree shopping, so Maisey got busy giving each station a last look over. One of her sitters had gone through each section to make sure every-thing was tidy for tomorrow and the place looked great. No one would ever know that many kids of various ages had come and gone through these sections today.

Six p.m. Ready. She got Chloe in her stroller and was heading to the door when Rex came through. Was he that good-looking yesterday? He wore jeans and a black leather jacket, a red plaid scarf around his neck.

He smiled a hello and played a round of peek-aboo with Chloe, who gave a gummy smile. "I borrowed an extra car seat from my sister and she helped me install it properly, so we're all set to go."

That was unexpected. Maisey was so used to not only doing everything for herself and Chloe, but thinking of everything. She liked that he'd not only thought of the car seat issue but that he'd installed it. Properly, no less. Now, *that* was an aphrodisiac. As was how he'd folded up Chloe's stroller and put it in the cargo area, then held her car door open for her. Little things that were actually big things when you wished you had more than two hands on a daily basis.

With Chloe settled in her rear-facing car seat, they headed off to the Christmas tree farm, driving past the ranch gates onto the long gravel road.

"So how'd you find the bottle with my letter to Santa, anyway?" she asked. Maisey had always wondered if someone had found it. Right after she'd tossed it in the creek and watched it get carried away by the fast-moving current, she'd been sure someone wonderful would find it and come get her, a family with children and pets. As the years wore on, she figured the bottle was still in the river. Turned out she was right about that.

"I was supposed to meet someone, a witness to a crime, on a park footbridge over the Bear Ridge River, but he didn't show."

"Yikes. Maybe he got scared? I don't really know how any of that works."

"Witnesses are definitely scared. They testify and get whisked off somewhere they've never been with a new identity. It's hard stuff. But the trial starts soon after the New Year. I need to find the witness before then."

"Sounds so stressful—for you, too."

He nodded. "Everything about it is stressful.

I like being a marshal and don't. Suited to it and not. Sounds nuts, right?"

"I kind of get it. A catch-22. You'd be crazy if you *did* like it."

He smiled. "Exactly. Anyway, because I was on that bridge at that exact time, I met River. My dog. My sort-of dog. He's the one that found your bottle. I saw a cute stray sniffing something and went to check it out. I got your bottle and my sister, Daisy, got the dog. That was a month ago."

"Why didn't you take him in?" she asked. She'd met River when she interviewed with Daisy Dawson at her farmhouse. He'd been curled in his dog bed and looked so sweet and content. She'd had no idea he'd found her bottle. Next time she saw him, she'd give him a good petting.

"I don't have anywhere to call home, not really. I keep a condo in Cheyenne but I'm rarely there. I live in hotels."

"So you're just here on vacation till Christmas?" she asked. That would make it easier not to fall for his gorgeous face and long, lean body. She loved his intense blue eyes and strong nose and jawline. His black leather jacket. Not to mention all the inside stuff. Like how kind he was. Generous. Thoughtful. He asked questions and listened, though granted, that came with the territory of his job. Still, he wasn't working now and he still asked and listened. She barely knew Rex Dawson but he made her feel...*seen.*

He'd be leaving town in less than two weeks. Knowing that, she couldn't possibly fall madly in love with him and get her heart handed to her. Unless she was stupid. *So don't be stupid*, she told herself. *Say thank you and move along, away from those blue eyes and how strong and sexy he looks.*

"Yup. Boss-ordered. Then I'm gone again."

"Good to know," she blurted out before she could stop herself.

He turned to look at her for a second. Oops—again. Why had she said that? She shouldn't have even thought it. Rex Dawson's comings and goings had nothing to do with her. *Because you didn't know he existed before 5:59 p.m. yesterday and now you're in his SUV, your baby in the back seat, on the way to choose a Christmas tree, his treat. Thanks to Rex, Chloe will have a Christmas tree tonight.*

But pulsating deep inside her was the fact that he'd found the bottle. In that one letter she'd so carefully rolled up and slid inside, he knew everything about her. That sounded crazy, but it was the way she felt. Her essence, summed up in Dear Santa. The yearning for a parent to take care of her, care *about* her, love her, want her. The *come get me, please. I don't belong here. I need a family.*

Saying she wasn't picky. That she didn't want to be greedy in the hope for a sibling in addition to a parent.

Maisey bit her lip and turned to look out the window. The man sitting beside her missed nothing. Not what was in that letter. And not now with her sudden obsession with the passing trees. She could feel him glancing at her.

"You okay?" he asked. "One thing you should know about me is that I'm an asker. In my job, you can't take anything for granted or think you know someone. You have to ask. And most times, when I do, the person cracks."

She felt something inside her shutter. And her eyes narrowed on him. "I certainly don't want to crack, Marshal."

He glanced at her. "Bad choice of words. In my profession, it means I got to the witness in a *good* way, got underneath the fear and earned their trust."

"I just want a tree for Chloe. I'm not interested in trusting a man who's leaving town the day after Christmas."

That got her another quick glance. "You're a straight shooter like me."

"Might as well be," she said. Suddenly she wanted to jump out of the car, grab Chloe and run.

Because dammit, he *had* cracked her. He'd gotten under her skin, where she let few people. He had her with that assessing gaze and understanding and kindness. The been-there-done-that aspect of his job that had him experience his share of awful, even if not directly. Then again, he'd said his father died. He knew about pain and loss firsthand.

"Are you close with your mom?" she asked, needing to change the subject.

His shoulders relaxed a bit, so he was clearly glad she had. "We speak once a week, but I don't get to see her often. She's living her dream down in Florida on a small farm with an orange orchard. She has a new husband she loves and who adores her, three dogs, four cats and a parrot she taught to say nice things to her. 'Squawk—you look so pretty today, Diana. Squawk—beautiful dress, Diana.'"

Maisey laughed. "We could all use that parrot."

He nodded. "We sure could."

"So you mentioned your dad died. I'm sorry. I certainly know how that feels."

"Last December, a few weeks before Christmas. We weren't close. He made that impossible for all six of his children." The shoulders tensed up again. "He basically drank himself to death."

"I'm so sorry," she said, noting the hard set of his jaw, the way he stared out the windshield.

"I'm sorry about your parents, Maisey. And you were so young. Clearly eight or under. Was it an accident?"

"Fire," she said, staring down at her lap, clasping and unclasping her now sweaty hands. "We had a small farm, just a couple of cows and goats. My mom liked to make her own dairy products and sell them at the farmers' market in town. She made her own labels, too. Baby Maisey was the name of her little business."

The gentle smile he sent was so full of sympathy that she almost lost it. *Do. Not. Cry*, she told herself.

"I was five years old and in the house with my mom," she went on. "My dad was in the barn. It was a few weeks before Christmas and a candle set the living room curtains on fire. My dad got me out and went back in for my mom but—" She stopped, tears stinging.

He slowed the car and pulled over onto the side of the road, took off his seat belt and angled to face her. "I'm so sorry." He took her hands and held them.

She closed her eyes for a second, needing the comfort and wishing she could reject it, but his hands felt good around hers. "I was so confused afterward. That they were gone. I didn't understand. There was no family to take me in, so I went into the foster care system and ended up in a home run by Meredith, who was very kind. I got lucky."

"I met her. She seemed very nice and caring."

"You met her?"

"In my quest to find you," he said. "I hope that doesn't seem intrusive. You mentioned her in the letter to Santa. So when I couldn't track you down by your name, I looked her up."

Huh. She didn't know he'd gone that far. "That's nice—that you went to the trouble to find me."

"I had to know what happened. I needed to know that everything worked out all right."

Except it didn't. Then or now. "Well, I do have my own little family with Chloe," she said, sucking in a breath. She didn't love talking about this. At all. "That first year I was at Miss Meredith's," she heard herself saying, "some of the young foster kids in the house, three and under, would be picked up by a social worker to meet with a prospective family, and they'd be adopted. I never even got that far." Sometimes, when she talked to Rex, it was like the words came from somewhere deep inside her and not of her own volition. Trick of the marshal trade? He could make people talk? He certainly wasn't pushy.

"I wonder why," he said. "You must have been remarkably cute as a kid."

She laughed. "Why do you say that?"

"Because you're so beautiful now," he said, and she saw his entire body go stiff as if that had come out of him not of *his* own volition. "Um, plus, based on the letter," he added very quickly, biting his lip, "you were a really nice, thoughtful kid."

Oh, Marshal, she thought. *You like me. That way.* She smiled, then tried to hide it. She couldn't get into a flirtatious situation with this man. *Playing. With. Red. Hot. Fire. Leaving town, remember?*

"We'd better get driving," she suggested. "Don't want all the good trees taken."

He smiled and signaled and pulled back onto the road.

There. Good. He wasn't so focused on her. Facing her. Seeing her expression. "And thank you for saying that. Both things," she added. When was the last time anyone said she was beautiful? "I was always very tall for my age, so at five I looked like I was eight, and by the time I was eleven, I was five foot nine. It's harder to get adopted as an older child. I used to wish I was petite, but I like my height now."

Her mom was five-nine, too, and Maisey had eventually learned to stand up straight and tall the way her mother had. *This is me.*

"My whole family is tall. Daisy's five-nine or

five-ten. And when River stands up on his back legs? Six feet at least."

She smiled. "He's such a pretty dog. I met him during my interview at Daisy's house. There are pictures of your family all over her refrigerator. You're so lucky you have five siblings."

"I do feel lucky about that," he said. "They're good people. Every last one. And the babies are cute, too."

"I met them all my first day," she said. "That adorable Danny came over to meet Chloe in the Kid Zone and said he wanted to babysit her."

"He's hilarious. I'm staying with Axel and his wife, Sadie—Danny's parents."

"Oh, there's the sign for the Christmas tree farm," she said, pointing.

He turned onto the gravel road, where several of the evergreens were lit up with white lights. "One rule about picking a tree," he said as he pulled into a spot. "It has to be spectacular. It has to make you think, This *is my tree. This is* Chloe's *first Christmas tree.*"

Two more weeks of this and she wasn't supposed to fall insanely in love?

Right.

Chapter Three

The tree *was* spectacular. And six-month-old Chloe, from her spot in the baby carrier attached to the front of her mom's wool coat, had chosen it. Rex and Maisey had walked up and down the rows at the Reed Family Christmas Tree Farm, Maisey stopping in front of a gorgeous Fraser fir, and Chloe had waved her hand at it and gurgled something unintelligible.

"Chloe has spoken!" Maisey said, laughing.

One of the employees came over and said they'd made a great choice and got out his camera, a new Polaroid. "Picture comes with every tree purchase. Nice to get a photo of your family at the farm."

Rex froze, aware that Maisey had the same strange look on her face that he must have had on his.

"I'd love a photo," Maisey said, breaking the tension.

"Gather close," the man said.

Rex stood at Maisey's side as close as he could without actually physically touching her, the tree behind him. The man snapped the photo, which slid out of the camera, and he waved it around to develop.

"There you go," he said, handing Rex the photo. "Beautiful family. That's one cute baby you two have."

"Aww, thanks," Maisey said with a big smile, not glancing at Rex even once.

The man made a few funny faces at Chloe, who stared at him with her big hazel eyes. "All rightie, then. Let's get this beauty on top of your vehicle."

Phew. Rex was glad to escape to that task.

We're not together, he wanted to tell the guy, a total stranger. *That's not my baby.*

Interesting how Maisey had said *thanks* with a smile.

Because she liked the idea of them being mistaken for being a family? Because there was little point in making a thing over correcting the guy, who'd been just making pleasantries?

She thanked him as he paid, and once the tree was secure on the roof of Rex's car, they headed back to Maisey's cabin, the photo in a cup holder in the console between their seats.

"So that was awkward," she said. "The man mistaking us for a family." She kind of snorted. Maybe he'd been wrong about thinking she'd liked it. She was just being nice back. She picked up the photo and looked at it quickly, then put it back.

"Well, I can see how he thought we were," he said. "Even if I can't imagine myself with a wife and child. Nice for others to think I'm—" He stopped talking. He was saying way too much as it was.

"You're what?" she asked, and he could feel her curiosity about what he'd been going to say.

"Like a regular person," he found himself telling her. "Your typical guy who plans to get married, buy a house, start a family. That I come off as that man always surprises me because inside I feel so removed from that."

He glanced over to find her tilting her head with an expression that said she was thinking, *Very interesting. I'm going to analyze you later.*

"So I have two big boxes of Christmas decorations in the trunk. We can have that tree decked out in a half hour."

Her face brightened. "Wow. I wasn't expecting that. Thank you again."

He smiled, a warmth hitting his chest. He liked doing things for her, helping her.

When they arrived at her cabin, she headed in to put Chloe to bed. He eyed the photo and put it in the glove compartment, then texted Axel to come give him a hand getting the tree in and set up. Just as Maisey came back out, Axel was driving up in one of the golf carts they used to get around the ranch. Axel's cabin was a good five miles from the main hub of the guest ranch.

"Hi again," she said to Axel. "How's that adorable Danny?"

Axel grinned. "Last I saw him, he was flying his stuffed superhero lion around the living room and over the tower of blocks he built. He's excited about going to the Kid Zone for a bit tomorrow."

"Can't wait to see him again," she said. "I'll go make sure the spot where I want the tree is all clear."

As Maisey went back in, Axel narrowed his eyes at Rex. "Um, what? How did this happen?"

"We kind of knew each other. Long story."

"I've got time," Axel said, undoing one of the bungee cords securing the tree.

"Well, since she didn't have a tree, I thought I'd take her to get one."

His brother stared at him, a grin forming. "I see."

"No, you do not," Rex whispered. "It's not like that. I'm leaving after Christmas. It's not like anything can happen between me and Maisey."

"Famous last words, brother," Axel said. "I said that and then I met a single mom with a toddler, and now I'm a dad with a baby on the way."

Rex swallowed, which Axel must have caught because he laughed.

Dammit. "Can we just get the tree inside?" Rex said with a scowl. "I've got two boxes of decorations in the back, too."

"Oh, do you," Axel said, the grin back.

His annoying brother helped him get the tree in the cabin in front of the living room windows where Maisey indicated.

"That's some tree," Axel said, staring up at it, then him, the glee still in his eyes. "I'll go bring in the boxes." He was quickly back with them and set them by the tree. "I'll leave you two to do the trimming. See you tomorrow at the Kid Zone, Maisey."

"Thanks for your help," Maisey said. Then Axel and his grin were gone.

"You look so much like your brother. Noah, too. Daisy's hair is lighter than both of yours, but you all look alike."

He nodded. "Dead ringers for our dad. Sometimes that gets us into trouble."

"How so?"

There he was again, telling her stuff he didn't mean to say. Why did he keep doing that?

"Let's put it this way—Bo Dawson didn't have much respect for wedding rings. He pissed off a lot of people, both men and women whose hearts and trusts and money he took. He was also an alcoholic and remembered very little of the crud he pulled. He inherited this ranch from his parents and within a year ran it into the ground. If I showed you pictures of what it looked like when we inherited it, you wouldn't believe it."

"So Christmastime must be very complicated for you, too," she said. "Since he died last December. He might not have been an easy person to care about, but I have no doubt you cared deeply. You and all your siblings."

For a second he could only nod. Bo Dawson had had his good points, though toward the last few years they were fewer and farther between. He'd always lived in the moment, which was sometimes a good quality and oftentimes his worst. He could be fun to be around, could charm a smile out of anyone. Even when he was disappointing someone, which was a constant, it was hard to walk away, to tell him it was the last straw. A couple of his siblings had reached that breaking point. So yeah, complicated.

"Exactly right" was all he could say about that to Maisey, who seemed to understand him a bit too well. "When he died, he left us the ranch, what was left of it, and wrote us all letters. Actually, some weren't quite letters. He left my oldest brother, Ford, a map of where he'd buried his mother's diary, which to this day Ford hasn't found. And he left Axel a list of addresses."

"What was yours?"

"A key, plain silver, no writing on it. I have no idea what it opens and there wasn't a letter with it. At first I thought the key must have opened the old front door to the farmhouse or the old gate, but it didn't work. I've tried it on just about every old lock that Noah kept around after the rebuilding."

"Maybe it's just symbolic? A metaphorical key à la welcoming you back home?"

Rex shook his head. "My dad was more literal. It opens something on this property, something he wanted me to find." He threw up his hands. "No idea what, though. Frustrating like he was."

She nodded. "How about some eggnog as we decorate the tree?"

"Feel free to spike it," he said.

She grinned. "I happen to have some Baileys Irish Cream." She disappeared into the kitchen, and just as she came back with two glass mugs, her cell phone rang. He took the glasses from her. "Ooh, it's the boss. Hi, Daisy... Nope, this is a great time to talk."

Rex couldn't help but notice Maisey's expression change from happy curiosity to something a lot like dread.

"Me? Well, um, hmm," she said. Then listened some more. "Well, of course you can count on me... Rex? He happens to be here right now helping me with my Christmas tree. I'll ask him... Okay. Thanks, Daisy. Bye."

"Should I even ask what that was about and how I came into the conversation?" He smiled, but she still seemed kind of shaken.

"Daisy said she realized today that all the kids presently at the ranch will be here through the day of the Christmas fair, which is in five days. She loves the idea of doing a kids' show of some sort, and I can have set rehearsal times during Kid Zone hours for any children, staff and guests who'd like to participate." She bit her lip. "I'm not sure... As you know, I'm not very Christmassy. And to be honest, this kind of thing—a big fair, kids—really might pull a lot of heavy sadness out of me, you know?"

"Pulling sadness out of you might be a good

thing, though, Maisey. If you can look at it that way, I mean."

She turned away a bit and shrugged. "I don't want to let your sister down. She's the reason I have this great job in the first place. And apparently a lot of kids are looking forward to being part of the fair. We can put on a short concert of kids' holiday songs that even your nephew can participate in at just two years old. The whole idea sounds adorable. I can handle that, right?"

"It depends. What was the 'I'll ask Rex' about?"

She smiled. "Daisy suggested I recruit you to help me with the kids' concert, since you're on vacation and all."

"Oh, did she?" Rex asked, good-naturedly rolling his eyes. "Of course I'll help. Sign me right up."

"Really? Just like that?"

"Just like that," he said.

She stared at him for a moment. "We have the same amount of Christmas spirit. I have none and you have a quarter to an eighth, so that's barely any. We're putting on the children's Christmas show?"

"Yes. Yes, we are. Because I have a plan for you, Maisey."

Say what? "A plan?"

"You're going to get back your Christmas

spirit. One hundred percent. That's my job till I leave."

Her face fell, not what he was expecting. Which was dopey of him. Christmas was hard on them both. Had been for years, much, much longer and more painfully for Maisey. Sometimes Rex could be as dense as his sister was always accusing him of being.

"Sorry," he said. "I'm overstepping." It was so…complicated, and not, at the same time.

"I can't get back my Christmas spirit, Rex. Pleasant thought as it is. Christmas to me means losing my parents. It means waiting year after year for Santa to come through with a family for me to join. It means a ragged hole so deep inside my chest that even seeing Chloe in a Santa hat can't fill it. She helps—don't get me wrong. But Christmas and I just aren't a pair. I love the idea of the show but…"

"I hear you. And if anything gets to be too much with the show, I'll be there to help take over."

Now her face really did fall. "Why are you so damned nice?" she asked, her eyes glistening. "Ugh, now I'm all emotional."

He smiled. "Multicolored lights or white?" he asked. "How's that for a subject change?"

"Perfect. Why don't we each take a long sip

of our spiked eggnog and then everything will be better."

He raised his glass and so did she. They clinked, held each other's gazes, and it took a lot to move his eyes off her pretty face, her eyes holding many different emotions.

I do want to give you back your Christmas spirit, Maisey. And I'm going to.

An hour later, Maisey sat on the sofa, Rex beside her, her attention split between the beautiful tree and the man. They'd wrapped red tinsel and white lights and hung multicolored balls, and had long finished their spiked eggnogs. Snowbell sat on the arm of the sofa, grooming her face.

"The tree is missing something," he said.

She looked over at it, the lights bright and the garland and tinsel so festive. The tree made all the difference in the formerly dull living room. "Looks great to me."

He shook his head. "Ornaments. All the decorations are the standard stuff. There are no personal ornaments."

Maisey picked up her eggnog and took a long sip. She was about to go down the ole memory lane and wasn't sure she wanted to. "When I first got married, I bought a ton of ornaments for our tree. Nothing pricey since we didn't have much money. And a few days later someone actually stole the tree right out of our trailer. Believe that?"

He grimaced. "I don't want to believe it."

"Want to know the worst part?" she asked.

"No," he said. He reached for her hand and gave it a squeeze. "But tell me."

"Before the fire, I was playing with two of the ornaments in the living room, making them have a conversation on the coffee table. There was a princess figure and a cat. The cat was Siamese and had the greenest eyes. The ornament was on the long side and slender, and I loved it so much."

"You lost it in the fire," he said, his expression so full of compassion.

She shook her head. "Nope. The cat ornament was in my hand when my dad came rushing in for me. I got out of the house with it. I lost it when that idiot thief stole the tree from the trailer."

"What the hell is wrong with people? Who does that? Who steals someone's Christmas tree?"

"There weren't any presents under it at least. But I lost the one thing I had left of my parents. My favorite ornament. Snowbell here isn't a Siamese, but she reminds me of the ornament with her green eyes and skinny face." She gave Snowbell a scratch behind her ears. When she'd found the cat as a stray during her pregnancy, she'd been so struck by a similarity in their faces. Or maybe it was just wishful thinking.

"Have you tried to find a replica of the ornament online?" he asked. "Not that it would be the same."

"Oh, I want it. Bad. There are cat ornaments, but I've never found that exact one. If there was one thing I would ever ask Santa for in a letter again, it would be that."

Snowbell moved from the arm of the sofa onto Maisey's lap. She petted the cat's back, earning a purr. Maisey was grateful for the distraction, something to take her thoughts off loss—and off Rex, sitting way too close despite being a good foot away. He reached over to pet Snowbell and their fingers collided. She felt it in her *toes*.

She wanted him to stay *and* go. Stay so she could be around him, look at him, talk to him. Go so she could get back her equilibrium and stop saying too much. Did she have to tell him about the ornament? The stuff that poured out of her mouth was nuts. Half of what she told Rex Dawson she'd never even told her husband when they were first married and she'd thought he'd cared.

"What do *you* want for Christmas?" she asked. There. She'd gotten the topic of conversation off herself and on to him. Not that she wanted to know too much about him. Every time he opened up to her, she found herself drawn closer and closer.

"To be assured I'll find my witness when I leave."

What, you were expecting him to say "To kiss you, Maisey Clark. Just one unforgettable kiss to remember you by that in fact will knock me off my feet so hard I don't leave"?

Right. She might not have much Christmas spirit, but the Christmas wishes ran deep.

"Speaking of leaving," he said. "I'd better get going." He stood up and gave Snowbell a final scratch by her tail.

Hmm. Suddenly he was dashing out the door. Maybe he didn't like talking about himself. Or maybe the whole evening had just been a lot. "Thanks for everything," she said. "The tree, the trimming…and listening."

"Anytime. So what time should I come by tomorrow for the kids' concert planning meeting?"

"Wow. You *are* an official," she said. This was a man who clearly took his responsibilities seriously, from finding his rogue witness to a children's holiday show. "How about my lunch break? It's just a half hour, but that should be enough to get the ball rolling. One p.m. in the cafeteria?"

"I'll see you then." He headed toward the door, giving the tree a glance. She also noticed that while he put on his leather jacket and wrapped the red plaid scarf around his neck, his gaze stopped on the photo of herself and her parents. Or maybe she'd imagined it, because he was suddenly saying goodbye and "Tell Chloe good-night for me if she wakes up during the night," which of course the 3:00 a.m. waker would, and then he was gone.

Maisey wanted him to come back immediately.

As Snowbell wound around her legs, she took in a breath. "I'm in trouble with this one," she told the cat.

She looked at the tree, marveling at what a difference it made in the cabin with its twinkling lights and red and silver balls hanging on the fragrant branches. When Maisey had been married, when she'd thought she'd finally have the family she always dreamed of, she'd tried to make their trailer as festive as possible at holiday time, but she realized she was overcompensating for everything wrong in her marriage, trying to wrap it in lights and bows and ornaments.

Everything that mattered, truly mattered, was sleeping in the nursery. She had to remember that and stop thinking about the guy who'd made this tree happen—the guy who'd be gone right after Christmas. And he was *not* taking her heart with him.

Chapter Four

If he were honest, Rex thought the next morning as he poured a cup of coffee in the quiet of his brother's kitchen, he would have told Maisey that what he wanted for Christmas was to restore her Christmas spirit. Granted, finding his witness was paramount and the need was always humming under the surface. If he could just reach the man, talk to him, Rex was sure he could convince him to come under protection, testify and then live a safe life in the witness protection program.

But his wish, his fervent wish, was to give Maisey back Christmas. For the girl she'd been, the woman she was.

And dammit, he was going to find that Siamese cat ornament. After all she'd been through, someone stole the last thing she had left of her parents? Attached to a Christmas tree? He shook his head for the zillionth time, disgusted by the creeps and criminals out there. Injustice, from the pettiest of crimes to the whoppers, always reinforced his dedication to his job and the US Marshals' motto: Justice. Integrity. Service.

Finding the ornament online was turning out to be as difficult as searching for Maisey and the witness had been. Nothing. There were plenty of Siamese cat ornaments, but none with green eyes or that were long and skinny. Luckily, he had a good idea of what it looked like. He'd been able to see it pretty clearly on the tree behind her and her parents in the photo on the console table in her hallway, which he'd noticed again as he'd been putting on his jacket last night.

And leaving, which he'd been loath to do.

What was it about this woman that pulled him in so hard? The letter to Santa? That she was all alone in the world with a baby? She was young, just twenty-three, but Maisey Clark was doing just fine. She was focused and independent, took care of business. Something about the combination of everything she was, including undeniably sexy, drew him like never before.

Except he wasn't open to a relationship. Or becoming a father. *So watch your step, Rex.* Even if Maisey would be open to dating short-term while he was here—which he doubted—he knew he could never think of her as a fling. She was already underneath his skin. She'd gotten there before he'd even *met* her.

He took a long gulp of coffee and a bite of the bagel he'd toasted and slathered with vegetable cream cheese, then opened up his laptop, planning to put in an hour checking into his witness's possible whereabouts, looking into credit card usage. When he logged in to his work site, a message greeted him from his boss. Vacation means vacation. See you on the twenty-sixth and not before—that goes for online, too. This is an order.

Rex shut his laptop, shaking his head. How was he going to put work out of his thoughts for the next week and a half without going nuts?

By focusing on what else you want: bringing back Maisey's Christmas spirit. And a perfect part of that plan would be taken care of by helping her with the concert. For the next bunch of days she'd be immersed in Christmas, which wouldn't be easy, and he'd be right there when it got rough, with a shoulder or an ear. Whatever she needed.

He had four hours until he'd meet Maisey at the caf, so he figured he'd do what he did in downtime at the ranch. Try a bunch of locks with the key his father had left him. Axel and Sadie, who'd joined the ranch staff when she'd married Axel and now served as the nutritionist, planning meals for guests with all kinds of restrictions, were both at work, and Danny was at the Kid Zone.

He called his brother Noah. As the one who'd rebuilt the ranch last winter and spring with a crew and now served as the general manager—his wife, Sara, was forewoman—Noah might be able to solve the key mystery. "Okay, there have to be a few other locks we haven't tried to open with my key. What are we missing?"

Noah had saved a lot of the old doors to the cabins and barns in case he wanted to repurpose them, but they'd tried all those. No dice. Last Christmas, when all the siblings had been home, they'd tried the attic, looking for anything with a lock among their dad's possessions, but except for a toolbox with an old lock on it that took a tiny key and a locked trunk they'd all been sure was the jackpot but wasn't, Rex hadn't found the key's purpose.

"Maybe the key doesn't open something on the ranch," Noah said. "Maybe you've been looking in the wrong place."

He'd been thinking about that lately. But where, then? And what? "So a safety-deposit box. A locker. But where? I don't even know where to start."

"Somewhere Dad must have frequented," Noah suggested.

Rex had no clue, though. He hadn't spent much time with his father the past few years before his death. His job had kept him away, but so had his memories. Maybe more so. His mother would drop off him and Axel and Zeke as kids after the divorce, and his dad would disappear, no food in the fridge. They'd call their eldest brother, Ford, who had a different mother, and Ford's mother would drop off takeout for them, shaking her head. If they called their own mother, they knew she'd be furious at how negligent Bo Dawson was, and they wouldn't be allowed back. Back then, they'd wanted to spend time with their dad any way they could, the good with the bad.

Once his dad married Daisy and Noah's mother and they'd come to visit, there were always delicious home-cooked meals. But she'd died when Rex was thirteen, and Bo had gotten worse. Noah and Daisy had truly been on their own as tweens and then teens. Rex knew that Noah's relationship with his father had been nothing short of turbulent. But he'd made peace with that this past year—which had helped Rex believe that anything was possible.

"Besides bars?" Rex asked.

"Maybe you *are* looking for a bar, Rex. Though I don't know why a bar would have lockers. Employee room, maybe? Oh—gotta go. Runaway goat with a group of kids cheering her on."

Hermione was the resident escape artist. No matter how strong Noah and Sara fortified her corral and her outdoor fence, she got out and ran for the hills. The only good news was that the guests loved it. The escape and the chase. Hermione could always be coaxed over with a bowl of hay with peaches in it.

"Good luck," Rex said.

"You, too. Start with Hot Rods, then try Wacky Dan's. Those were his two favorites. Who knows?"

Words to live by. Rex put his phone away and made a plan to stop by both bars tonight. He'd drag one of his siblings with him. In the meantime, he'd go help his brother corral the runaway goat.

The moment Maisey walked into the cafeteria, the O'Leary kids raced up to her, seven-year-old Lara throwing her arms around Maisey's waist, five-year-old Sam holding out his brownie and asking if Maisey wanted a piece, but only a little piece, which made her laugh, and three-year-old

Tommy simply clapping at her side as though she were a movie star.

She could get used to this. The children were the one part of the Christmas show that made it all seem doable instead of potentially painful. These kids were joyful, bursting with life, and would make even having a spare moment to think about her own losses and sad times just about impossible. She hoped, anyway.

"Hi, Maisey," called adorable Jack Lopez from his table with his parents, ten years old and a budding scientist. His younger sister, Kyra, sat reading a Harry Potter book that probably weighed more than she did. Kyra looked up and grinned at Maisey.

Huh. This was a lot different from the reception she was used to at the day care. The kids there had liked her a lot, sure, but here, she was the "special grown-up" in the Kid Zone who was all about fun. The kids adored the two staffers, too, high-energy young adults whom Maisey adored herself.

How did I get so lucky? she asked herself as she sat at a back table, accepting a big hug from the eight-year-old Caletti twins, Amelia and Ava, on their way out. Tyler, the teenage basketball player, gave her a high five as he left, but Zara, glum as always, walked right past her. The girl gave her a glance but not a smile or a hello. Her parents smiled tightly at Maisey, and she was too curious what the deal was with the dynamic. Something must have happened in the family. But unless one of the Harwoods opened up to her, she couldn't exactly just ask.

Rex came in, filling the doorway with his six-foot-two, long, lean but muscular hot physique as he glanced around for her. As his gaze stopped on her, tingles zapped along her spine.

She sprang up because of butterflies zapping around her stomach. "Shall we hit the line?" she asked, gesturing at the front of the cafeteria, where a few guests and several staff members were making their choices. "I hear the loaded potato soup is amazing. I think I might go for that and the half sandwich combo. Maybe a BLT. Or turkey. Or a turkey BLT."

Oh, Lord. Shut up, Motormouth Maisey. Were there women who were effortlessly sophisticated and alluring and full of mystery when she was talking about turkey sandwiches? Then again, the less "hot" she was in his eyes, the better. She didn't want him to be interested in her that way. Knowing he was attracted might give her a little ego boost, but she certainly wasn't looking to get involved with anyone, let alone a man who was leaving in less than two weeks. *We've been through this, Maisey*, she told herself with a firm mental conk on the head.

"Potato soup might be just what the doc ordered—wind is whipping out there today."

Yup. And the reason why the Kid Zone had been packed this morning. Almost all the guests and staff kids had been in, whether for an hour or all morning. When it got truly cold but there wasn't enough snow for cross-country skiing or snowshoeing, the indoor petting zoo and lodge activities were the best bets. When kids got their fill of petting the goats and marveling over the llamas and the rehabilitating reindeer, they headed into the Kid Zone.

They were standing very close in the cafeteria line, burgers and fries ready to go, sandwiches made to order, a soup and salad bar, and then the day's specials. She and Rex both got the soup-and-sandwich combo, a BLT for her and a turkey club for Rex. Back at the table, they dug in to their lunch, but since she only had a half hour, they had to get down to business.

Maisey pulled out her handy small notebook and a pen. "Okay. Children's holiday concert—which is four days from now. I have a little experience with this from the day care where I worked. Because we have mostly young kids, I'm thinking we put on a concert for the parents with, say, five songs, kids in adorable costumes with fun holiday props. All the kids involved who want to be. Parents can sign them up and drop them off at a set time for rehearsals every day."

He lifted the second half of his sandwich. "Sounds great, Maisey. I'll be your right-hand man, builder, set designer. Anything you need."

A kiss. Right now.

Oh, man. Where had that come from? She knew where. From how close they were sitting, working together…

"You two are under the mistletoe, so you have to kiss," a voice said.

Maisey whirled around. Fourteen-year-old Annalise Vega stood on a chair behind them, holding up a sprig of mistletoe tied with a red-and-green plaid ribbon over their heads.

"Kiss, kiss, kiss, kiss!" she called out.

The entire cafeteria, not that there were so many people left, began chanting and clapping.

"I don't think they'll stop until we kiss," Rex said.

"A quick peck, then. On three."

He kissed her on two. Warm, fast and leaving her wanting more. How could she have possibly felt that kiss along her spine, across the nape of her neck? But she had. Tingles.

"Just where did you get that, anyway?" Maisey asked Annalise.

"Found it in our welcome basket when we arrived. My mom told me it was mistletoe, the kissing plant. Whoever stands under it has to kiss." Annalise giggled and blew them a kiss, then ran off.

"So we have my sister, the guest relations manager, to blame for this," Rex said.

A big part of Maisey wanted to thank her boss. She liked that kiss.

"You'll text me about what you need for the show?" he asked. "I'm all yours, seriously, so load me up with tasks."

All hers. When he said stuff like that, she immediately found herself fantasizing about a different Maisey living an alternate life, one in which she trusted people, trusted romance. One where the man she found so sexy and alluring and kind and generous would be sticking around.

"I will," she said. "And thank you." She glanced at the clock on the wall. "Time for me to get back to the lodge."

"I'll walk you," he said with an easy smile.

Sigh. Of course he would.

Because he was fast seeming like everything she'd ever wanted in a man, a husband, a life partner.

Chapter Five

By late afternoon, Maisey had spoken to just about all the parents who'd either dropped off or picked up their children in the Kid Zone. All were on board for having their kids in the holiday show. Rehearsals would be every morning at nine thirty so that the children could have a half hour of unstructured playtime first and then get into singing mode. So far, this was coming together without a hitch. They'd only have four days to create magic, but kid magic was its own special kind. Even with flubs and forgotten lyrics, the show would be special and fun for everyone—most important, the young participants.

"I knew you'd pull this off in no time," Daisy Dawson said, coming over to where Maisey stood in the baby-and-toddler section. Tony, Daisy's five-month-old son, and her brother Noah's eight-month-old twins were all napping in bassinets a few feet away, a lullaby player on low. Somehow, the ambient noises of the Kid Zone helped put all the littlest ones down when it was time for their naps, and the loudest ball dribblings and happy screams didn't awaken them. Axel's son, Danny, was jumping in the small ball pit with another toddler. Hannah, one of the Kid Zone sitters, was supervising them while Maisey spoke to her boss. They could clearly hear the toddlers singing the one line they'd learned from a song, "Frosty the Snowman." Which was more like "Frotty Noman" over and over between giggles.

Between lunch with Rex and coming back to work, she'd created a song list, starting with "Frosty" and ending with "All I Want for Christmas Is My Two Front Teeth." All the kids thought that was funny.

"The show will be adorable," Maisey said. "And I can really focus on rehearsals and getting the kids ready for the big day because your brother Rex has agreed to be my set builder, costume designer and all-around right-hand guy."

Daisy beamed, twirling the end of her long

brown ponytail around her finger. "Oh, has he?" She leaned a bit closer to whisper, "You do realize that's unusual for Rex. Or maybe you don't since you're new around here. It's *very* unusual."

Hmm, a little matchmaking going on here? Rex's sister definitely wanted her to know that Rex didn't go around offering to help with kiddie holiday shows.

The happy goose bumps that had run up her spine started fading. "Even if I were in the market for a relationship, which I'm not for a million reasons," Maisey said, "he's made it very clear he's leaving town the day after Christmas."

"Ha—I've heard that one before. Noah, Axel and I are all proof that definitive statements about ourselves and our plans are poppycock."

Maisey laughed. "That's sort of good to know. Maybe I'm not totally cynical about love at twenty-three even though I feel like I should be. I've already got a failed marriage."

Daisy glanced around to make sure no little ears were in hearing distance. "You're talking to someone whose first fiancé, Tony's biological father, left her at the altar. Literally. He sent me a Dear Jane text five minutes before the wedding. A half hour later I went into labor on the side of a service road out in the middle of nowhere. A guest at the ranch, a man I hadn't yet met, came along and helped bring my baby, Tony, into the world. We're married now."

Maisey's eyes popped. "Wow."

"My trust level those early days and weeks of knowing Harrison McCord? Zero. But when love conks you over the head, there's no running from it."

Maisey grinned. "I suppose not. Probably wouldn't get very far with a serious conk."

"That's it exactly. Rex can try leaving, but it'll be futile."

Hmm. Maisey came from the school of *when someone tells you something about them, believe them.* Could she loosen up a little and see where things with Rex Dawson might lead? She'd just have to take it day by day. Moment by moment, actually.

A text pinged on Daisy's phone. "Guest emergency," she said. "Emergency meaning Cabin Four is out of paper towels and one of the kids spilled his lemonade all over the floor. Let me go give my little guy one last peek before I skedaddle." She walked over to Tony's bassinet and gently kissed his head. "See you later, love," she said to her son. On her way out, she added, "And who knows, Maisey—we just might be family by New Year's."

Maisey smiled but her stomach was churning.

Family. Family. Family. What she would give to be part of a family like the Dawsons. But the last time she got hopeful about joining a family, she'd been sorely disappointed. Besides, she and Rex weren't even a thing. They were just…friends, really, who happened to share one electric kiss under the mistletoe in a cafeteria. Was it even a kiss? A peck. It was a peck. She'd better stop daydreaming that there was anything going on with her and Rex, because there wasn't. Daisy's hopeful words aside, Rex seemed very sure of his plans—to leave. To go back to his world as a US marshal.

"Emily signed me up to be in the show, but I'm not doing it," a voice muttered.

Maisey had been so wrapped up in her thoughts that she hadn't even seen nine-year-old Zara Harwood walk up beside her. The girl's arms were crossed over her chest, her chin lifted and her expression half sad, half defiant.

Then her mind caught on the name Emily. Maisey distinctly recalled the Harwoods, Emily and Ethan, referred to Zara as their daughter. But Zara referred to her mother as Emily? If Zara were fourteen or fifteen, Maisey would chalk it up to teenage rebellion. But Zara was only nine.

"Well, if you don't want to sing in the show," Maisey said, "you don't have to, but I would love it if you did. I was hoping you'd be one of my special apprentices, too."

Zara tilted her head, the grim expression softening. "What's an apprentice?"

"A very important helper. An assistant. It's a special job. We have ten kids in the show, including you if you decide to be in it. Several are really young and I need extra-special assistance with helping them learn the songs. I've seen you carrying your iPod with your earbuds in, so I figured, *Now, there's a girl who really likes music.* You'd be a big help to me."

"Really? I could do that." Zara bit her lip, the hands coming out of her pockets.

Thank you, universe. Maisey had only been half-sure the girl wasn't going to tell her she didn't want to help with "her dumb show" and go storming off.

"Can you tell me what songs we're doing?" Zara asked. "I want to download them."

Maisey could jump up and down in joy. Yes! She told the girl the songs and Zara scampered off to a beanbag.

A few minutes later, Emily Harwood came in, and this time, Zara ran over to her.

"Guess what? I'm going to be a special app—" She turned to Maisey. "What is it called again? The special assistant?"

"Apprentice," Maisey said.

"I'm going to be a special apprentice for the kids' holiday show," Zara told Emily. "I might be in the show, too. I haven't decided yet."

"That's so great!" Emily said. "I hope you'll be in the show, too. You have such a beautiful voice."

Zara's face fell. Why, given the compliment, Maisey had no idea. "I said I don't know yet."

"Well, it's great that you're going to be an apprentice." Emily glanced at her watch. "It's time for your horseback riding lesson. All ready?"

Zara nodded and went to her cubby to put on her boots and jacket.

"Oh my gosh, thank you," Emily whispered to Maisey. "You have no idea how helpful this is for her and us as a family."

Maisey was dying to ask why exactly, but she couldn't pry. If Zara or Emily wanted to share, they would. Maisey had always hated being asked about her situation when she was a kid. Even when someone asked something as simple as "Where did you grow up?" Maisey would get a stomachache. Yes, she'd grown up in Prairie City—before and after her parents' deaths. But the real answer seemed less like a place and more like, *I grew up in a few different Prairie City group foster homes*. Once, she'd said that and the person, who'd just been making small talk, had practically run away in discomfort.

Maisey watched the pair leave, buoyed by how differently Zara was carrying herself. No slumped shoulders or trailing behind. She was talking to Emily for once, too. As they disappeared through the double doors, in walked Rex Dawson. Maisey wasn't one to exaggerate, but the world seemed to move in slow motion and he sauntered over to her in his black leather jacket and sexy jeans and brown cowboy boots.

"I hear all my nieces and nephews are in one place, so I thought I'd come visit them," he said.

She had a feeling his sister would say that also wasn't something he usually did. Maybe Rex Dawson had a crush on her, too. Now she sounded like the twenty-three-year-old she was. Did thirty-one-year-old men have crushes? Maybe.

"Well, your baby niece and nephews are all sleeping over there," she said. "But Danny appears to be building a skyscraper out of big blocks." She pointed to where the toddler sat, tongue out in fierce concentration as he added another foam block to the top of his tall tower. Hannah gave him a high five.

"Nice building!" Rex said, walking over. "It's taller than you!"

Maisey noted how Danny's adorable face lit

up at the sight of his uncle. He came racing over, flinging himself into Rex's arms. Rex lifted him high, then dangled him upside down and sideways before giving him a big hug. Danny was full of giggles.

"Knock down tower?" Danny asked Hannah.

"Go for it!" the sitter said.

Danny took a running leap and crashed through the tower. Then he and Rex scooped up the blocks into their basket. The boy let out a giant yawn. Then another.

"Someone's ready for his nap," Maisey said, holding out her hand. "Your mat and favorite blankie and lovey are all ready." She held out his stuffed lion wearing a red cape.

"Want to hear a story before nap time, Dan the man?" Rex asked.

Danny grinned. "Yes! Zul souphero lion!"

"You got it," Rex said, carrying Danny over to the nap area and the navy blue mats behind a curtain.

Danny let out a giant yawn and then the two disappeared from view. Maisey stood just to the side of the curtain, taking a peek in. Rex was taking off Danny's sneakers. Then he settled the boy under the superhero blanket, a little pillow under his head, and sat beside him as he started a story about his stuffed superhero lion.

Maisey heard a big yawn. Then Rex continued the story. Then silence. A few seconds later, Rex emerged. "Asleep in three seconds," he whispered.

"A record for sure." Maisey felt so tongue-tied as she just stared at Rex like a fool, unable to look away from his gorgeous face and blue eyes and that incredible body. The guy had her completely hooked now. Kind and generous with his time? Check. Trying to give her back the Christmas spirit she'd lost a long, long time ago? Double check. Sweet and gentle with little kids? Be still, her heart.

She was now in official trouble, her head and heart in serious jeopardy. No matter what Daisy said, Rex had said quite a few times he was leaving after Christmas. The next time someone dangled mistletoe over their heads, she'd have to go running.

"So this was Dad's favorite bar?" Rex asked Axel as they walked into Hot Rods, located at the end of Main Street in Bear Ridge. Some people were at tables, drinking beer. A waitress was delivering two plates of fried something to a couple who were lip-locked even as she set down the food. A couple of guys were playing pool.

"Apparently," Axel said. "Meets all the requirements. Pool table, dartboard, long bar, jukebox, free peanuts, even a dance floor for his hookups."

There were two couples slow dancing to an old Eric Clapton song. He could well imagine his dad, hanging heavily on the woman he'd met, sloshed out of his mind.

Axel ordered them two draft beers, and Rex cracked open a peanut from the bowl full of them and popped it in his mouth. As the bartender set down the beers, Rex said to him, "Our dad used to come here a lot and we think maybe this key—" he fished it out of his pocket and held it up "—might open something here. Locker?"

The bartender eyed the small key. "There are some lockers in the employee lounge, but they have combination locks. And that key wouldn't fit either the front or back door." He shrugged.

"Well, this was a long shot," Rex said. "But thanks."

As the bartender helped another set of customers, Axel took a sip of his beer. "We can check out Wacky Dan's. After I beat you at darts."

"You mean after I wipe the sticky, peanut-shell-covered floor with you," Rex said with a grin. They ordered a platter of mozzarella sticks to share, then headed over to the dartboard just as a Bon Jovi song came blaring on the juke-box, bringing up more dancing couples. A trio of middle-aged women came in, and several eyes turned toward them, beer guts getting sucked in, hair getting smoothed back. This place was definitely more couples-oriented and pickup-ish than Rex had expected. He'd pictured lonely, drunk men half slumped on the bar, getting into fights and passing out on the floor. Bo Dawson had been a ladies' man till the end, so Rex supposed this being his favorite bar wasn't all that surprising. He probably met most of his girlfriends here.

"What do you think Dad might have left you?" Axel asked, taking aim at the board and hitting very close to the bull's-eye.

Rex shrugged. "I've spent the past year trying to figure it out and I can't even imagine. I seriously can't come up with anything. I think of all of us, I was maybe the least close to him."

"Yeah? Why do you say that? I'd think Zeke would say that about himself. And definitely Ford."

Zeke, a successful businessman in Cheyenne, had left town when he graduated from high school and barely looked back. Growing up, Zeke had kept his head down and focused on his schoolwork, determined to find a way out of the future Bo Dawson seemed to lay in front of them. Ford, their eldest brother, definitely had his share of problems with Bo Dawson.

"Yeah, good point," Rex said. "And the main reason Ford would say that is because he's a cop and Dad liked to skirt the law. Dad would see him coming for a visit and make himself scarce. Ford told me outright about those times and how it made him feel. But they were close once, when Ford was a kid. Dad and I never were. Never talked."

"Why do you think that was?" Axel asked, pausing with the dart in his hand.

"Once, when I was fifteen, he said, 'You're the kid who's gonna move far, far away and we'll never see you again.' Which shocked the hell out of me because I realized how well he did know me. All I could think about back then was leaving and going far, far away."

"Huh, interesting. So maybe the key you've been searching for is metaphorical, like Daisy suggested. Maybe it's not to anything but just refers to you having a key back to the Dawson Family Guest Ranch."

"Yeah, maybe. I just don't think so, though. That wasn't really Dad's style. He was more in your face with what he wanted us to know."

Axel shot his dart. Close again but no cigar. "Agreed. The list of five addresses he left me was plenty in my face."

Rex had joined Axel on the last address he had

left to visit back in the summer. Each of the addresses had shed light on Bo Dawson—from his childhood, to a family he'd been generous with, to an old girlfriend who'd helped Axel understand Bo better, make peace with his complicated feelings. Rex had always thought his brother was a real lone wolf, a former search-and-rescue operative who'd come home to take charge of guest safety and lead wilderness tours for the ranch. Suddenly the guy was married to his perfect match and they shared a two-year-old Rex adored and were expecting a baby.

As the waitress plunked down the platter of mozzarella sticks on the table holding their beers, Rex thought about how if Daisy had her way, the key and what it unlocked would lead him back home for good, too—to settle down and get married. *Married, married, married.* The word echoed in his head, sounding foreign or made up, something that couldn't possibly apply to him.

But then Maisey, with her long blond hair and pale brown eyes, and baby Chloe, with her big hazel-ish eyes and bear-ears hooded fleece snowsuit, came to mind. As did the old bottle he'd found and the letter to Santa. The tree they'd trimmed.

The two-second kiss under that sprig of mistletoe in a well-lit cafeteria at midday.

He'd felt that kiss *everywhere.*

Not a surprise, given how attracted he was to Maisey on so many levels.

Axel flew a dart, this time landing right in the bull's-eye. "Ah, success." He took a slug of his beer and made quick work of a mozzarella stick slathered in hot sauce, then another. Rex grabbed one before his brother ate the whole plate. "So what's going on with you and Maisey?"

Oh, crud. "I'm helping her with the kids' holiday show. That's what's going on."

Axel's smile was slow and wide. "Sure, Rex. Because you do that kind of thing."

"Maisey and I have history."

Axel downed another mozzarella stick. "How? She's been at the ranch, like, three days."

"A month ago, when I found River poking around the water's edge at the nature preserve, he'd been sniffing an old bottle. Turns out there was a message inside. A letter to Santa dated fifteen years ago."

"And?" Axel said, taking a sip of his beer.

"And it was signed Maisey Clark. I tried everything to find her because I had to know if she got what she'd asked Santa for. But I couldn't track her down. Then Daisy tells me she's the new Kid Zone nanny."

Axel shook his head. "Wow. That's some crazy coincidence. Like you were meant to know her."

"Or to find out what happened—if she got her wish."

"Did she?" Axel asked.

"Nope. I'm here till the day after Christmas and I want to give her back her Christmas spirit. Give her and her baby daughter a good holiday. That's all this is about."

The slow, wide smile was back. "And you like her."

That kiss came to mind. The feel of Maisey's soft lips. The slight scent of a floral perfume. And all the other…stuff the kiss had engendered. "So I like her. I'm still leaving. Day after Christmas. I've got a complicated case to deal with. And a marshal's life is on the road, hotel after hotel. I live out of a suitcase."

"I'd think that would have gotten old by now."

Rex sighed inwardly. It had. But he still felt deeply committed to his job. He believed in what he did. He rarely thought about what had driven him to become a marshal—a very old case involving a frenemy of his dad's who'd turned to armed robbery and escaped custody. Bo Dawson had swindled the guy in a blackjack game right before he'd been arrested, and they'd all been sure—as kids and teenagers—that the criminal would come after them for revenge. The US Marshals Service had caught the man a day later, but the fear, the worry, the instinct to protect those he loved, had stuck with Rex. He'd had to become a cop first, but then he'd set his sights on the US Marshals to chase down fugitives.

"You'll be back, bro. I'll put money on it."

Not an option, he thought, but Axel had hit another bull's-eye, then another and was busy gloating, so Rex didn't have to argue. He didn't really have the argument in him; the feeling was just *there*, deep inside.

"Wanna hit up Wacky Dan's and see if they have lockers that take keys? It was Dad's other home away from home."

"Another time," Rex said, grabbing a dart and needing to hit the center. If he did, he'd feel less off-kilter, and all his wayward thoughts—about Maisey mostly—would fall into line. He aimed, he shot... The dart barely stuck and landed on the floor.

"That means I get the last mozzarella stick," Axel said, snatching it up.

Rex laughed, glad to know some things never changed, like brothers. Everything else in his life seemed so unsettled, even though nothing really was. He'd leave soon, find his witness, take his next case.

It's the soft stuff inside your chest that's got you out of whack, he realized. And a woman and a baby he couldn't stop thinking about, wanted to help, protect, care for.

The sound of a spoon hitting a glass over and over many times snapped Rex from his thoughts. Half the place was clinking their glasses, grinning and chanting toward a couple on the dance floor.

"Mistle-toe, mistle-toe," they were chanting.

Rex glanced up, and sure enough, a sprig tied with red ribbon dangled from a hook in the ceiling right above the couple's heads. The couple gave the bar quite a show, to claps and cheers.

He had to admit he'd heard something of a parade in his head after that short, sweet kiss with Maisey in the cafeteria. Over in two seconds, but the clangs of cymbals nonetheless.

Serious physical attraction and caring about someone equaled danger, as far as he was concerned. But he had no idea how to possibly step back.

Chapter Six

In the morning, Maisey was over on the far side of the Kid Zone, which had been turned into the Dawson Family Guest Ranch Children's Holiday Show central. The kids had worked hard on lining up and taping together six big poster boards to create a huge backdrop that would hang from two hooks on the ceiling above the stage. Thanks to two artistic teens, Tyler and Annalise, who'd penciled in the name of the show surrounded by little Santas, Mrs. Clauses, elves, reindeer and candy canes, the festive banner was being painted by kids of all ages. Maisey had carefully taped it onto the mat flooring so that the kids could easily work from all sides without shifting the banner around.

"Oops," said five-year-old Sam O'Leary. "I got red paint out of the lines on my *H*."

Maisey glanced over at where Sam was lying on his belly, propped up on his elbows in front of the *H* in *Holiday*, a paintbrush in his hand and a frown on his adorably freckled face. She was about to tell him that was absolutely fine when Zara Harwood, Maisey's song apprentice, scooted over and looked at Sam's handiwork.

"I know!" Zara said, pushing her brown ponytail over her shoulder. "If you make that part of the *H* a little wider, no one will know you painted out of the line."

Sam brightened as he looked at Zara, then dipped his paintbrush into the red paint, widening his *H*. "It worked!"

"Awesome," Zara said, looking quite pleased with herself and rightly so.

Maisey wanted to scream with happiness. Since she'd started working here four days ago, Zara had barely said five words. Now she was engaged, working collaboratively and being a real sweetheart to the younger kids.

"High five!' Maisey whispered to Zara, holding up her hand with an appreciative smile.

Zara grinned and gave her five, her hazel eyes so happy, then went back to painting in an elf.

Huh. Maybe working on the kids' show would be an unexpected blessing instead of the potentially painful experience Maisey had feared. So far, she was so busy rehearsing songs and teaching lyrics and coming up with set ideas, plus taking care of Chloe, that she hadn't had much time to think about her own complicated feelings about Christmas. So far, so good.

"So what are you asking Santa for?" thirteen-year-old Tyler, who'd finally stopped dribbling and shooting to help paint, asked Annalise, whom he seemed to have a huge crush on. His moony-eyed staring was a clear giveaway.

Annalise looked up from where she was painting a reindeer. She shot Tyler a grin. "World peace and AirPods Pro."

His mouth dropped open. "Hey, me, too! And the two pairs of new sneakers I want. And basketball camp this summer."

"I'm asking for a kitten," eight-year-old Ava Caletti announced.

"Me, too!" her sister, Amelia, added. "They're gonna be twins like us!"

Maisey adored the Caletti twins. They both had flame-red long hair in braids and green eyes and liked wearing brightly colored leggings with long T-shirts.

Ava nodded. "But not identical probably. I want mine to be orange."

"I want a black kitten with white paws."

"What are you asking for, Zara?" Annalise asked, moving to the other side of the banner to start painting a Mrs. Claus.

"Nothing, okay?" Zara snapped. "What's the stupid point? I never get what I ask Santa for, anyway." She threw down her pencil and stalked off, flopping herself on a beanbag.

Annalise frowned and glanced toward Zara, then at Maisey. "Sorry."

"Hey, it's all right," Maisey told the teenager. "It's a perfectly reasonable question to ask someone this time of year and it's what the group was talking about."

That seemed to make Annalise feel better and she got back to painting, Tyler filling up the silence by waxing on about how "vital the noise-canceling feature in the new AirPods Pro is."

Since the kids were all talking and working, Maisey nodded to Hannah, one of the sitters, to take over supervision while she walked over to Zara. She slid a nearby beanbag next to the girl's and sat down, hoping she'd actually be able to get up. Maisey might be young, but since she'd had a baby six months ago, her body still wasn't what it used to be.

"Every year, starting from when I was five," Maisey said, "I'd write Santa a letter asking for the same thing. I never got it. Once, I even put my letter in a bottle and threw it in the creek, hoping it would get to the north pole faster."

Zara looked up at Maisey, her eyes red rimmed. "So I'm right. Wishes don't come true. Or my mom and dad would have come back to life."

Oh, no. Maisey felt her eyes well up. "My parents died when I was young, too. I'm so sorry, Zara."

Zara stared at her but didn't say anything, then looked away. Finally, she added, "It's been more than a whole year and I don't know anyone else whose mom and dad died. Except you now. I mean, there are some kids at school whose mom died or their dad died, but not both. Emily and Ethan think it's good for me to go to a talk group of kids who lost parents, but I hate it. At least those kids still have a parent."

Emily and Ethan. Not Mom and Dad. Maisey knew she had to tread carefully with what she said to Zara without speaking to the Harwoods first, but she could certainly be compassionate even though she didn't have even a quarter of the story here. From the little she knew, she figured the Harwoods had adopted Zara and that Zara wasn't yet on board.

"I know what you mean," Maisey said. "When I was in my foster home, there were a couple kids there whose parents were alive but had problems and couldn't take care of them. I used to think, *At least their parents are alive*. But once I got older I realized loss is loss is loss and hurt is hurt. We used to talk about how we felt and it did make me feel better."

"Well, I hate it."

Maisey nodded, wishing she had the right words, magic words.

Zara looked up at her. "You were in a foster home? Were the parents nice to you?"

"I lived in three different group foster homes. And yes, the people who ran them were nice. I was pretty lucky in that regard."

Zara stared at her. "Emily and Ethan were friends with my mom and dad, so they became my parents right after—" She stopped talking, biting her lip and looking away. "I don't think I would have liked to live in a foster home," she added on a whisper. "So did you ever get *any-thing* you wished for for Christmas?"

Maisey smiled. "Yeah. I guess I did. Not exactly what I asked for, but in its own way, you know?"

Zara shrugged. "I want only what I want."

Maisey gave Zara's hand a squeeze. "I get it."

"Do you think I'm a good painter?" Zara asked.

Phew. This was a much easier topic of conversation. "Very good. I love the color choices for the elf you were working on. Very original and interesting. You put your own stamp on it."

Zara smiled. "I really like painting."

"Wanna go back over and keep working on it? I think you only have the big elf shoes left to do."

Zara brightened and stood, and as expected, it took Maisey a good thirty seconds to lug herself up. "I'm gonna do polka dots on one shoe and stripes on the other. Red and green."

"Love it," Maisey said with a nod.

Zara ran back over to the banner and picked up a paintbrush. Annalise gave her a smile. Then Zara smiled back.

Maisey let out a giant breath, then almost sucked it back in when Rex Dawson walked through the door in his sexy leather jacket, the red plaid scarf around his neck. She tried not to stare as he took off his coat and hung it on a chair, the scarf following. *Keep going*, she wanted to say. *The shirt next...*

This guy might want to give me back Christmas, which I'm not sure is possible, but he's definitely given me back my mojo. She truly hadn't been sure she'd ever see that again.

As he walked over, Tyler got up and grabbed

his basketball and dribbled up to Rex, blocking his path, dribbling the ball on either side of his legs. "Freestyle. Whoever scores a point first is crowned king of the lodge."

"You're on," Rex said.

Tyler dribbled and Rex crouched as if to block his shot, but it was clear he wasn't trying—he also had a good foot on Tyler, who hadn't hit his growth spurt. The ball went in. "Yeah! King of the lodge!"

"Oh, yeah, watch this," Rex said, spinning around and shooting with one hand. The ball went in.

Tyler's mouth dropped open. "Whaaaa?"

Rex laughed. "I got moves for someone over thirty. Barely over, but over."

"Yeah, you do," Tyler said, reverence in his voice.

"Tell you what. I need to start building the set for the holiday show. But how about we play a pickup game in about an hour if you're still here. If not, I'll catch you tomorrow."

Tyler grinned. "Awesome." He dribbled his way back to the painting crew, wedging his way in beside Annalise.

Maisey smiled, her heart annoying her with its pitter-patter. "That was nice of you."

Rex gave half a shrug. "Teenagers are fun. Especially when they're not yours."

She smiled until what he said hit her. Really hit

her. He didn't want to be a parent. Even though he'd be such a great one! *The man does not want to be a dad. Get it through your head.*

And guess what you are and love being: a mom.

You have to stop thinking about Rex Dawson as a possibility. He's not.

The disappointment slugged her hard in the stomach to the point that she winced. She was grateful for the distraction of little Lara O'Leary somehow ending up with her paintbrush full of purple paint getting stuck in her curly blond hair.

"Oopsies!" Lara said, giggling.

The kids' reactions ran the gamut from laughter to dropped-mouth awe.

"Paint crisis," Maisey said to Rex. "Back in a minute." She hurried over to the little girl, catching her breath from the whirlwind that was Rex Dawson. Luckily, the paint was water based and would come out with a little muscle and a paper towel with some soap.

But Hannah already had the paintbrush out of the girl's hair. "I'll take her to the sink station. I got green paint in my own hair yesterday and it came right out."

"I like having purple hair," Lara said, looking at the ends of her long curly hair with a big grin.

The two walked off toward the "cleanup station," which had a sink, soap and hand sanitizer.

"Now, that's my kind of crisis," Rex said. "I could get used to that. A little water-soluble paint in hair." He chuckled.

"If your sister were here, she'd say that life could be yours with a snap of your fingers. Just come work at the ranch."

"Ah, I see you do know Daisy pretty well." He grinned but the big smile didn't last.

He really doesn't want to be here, she thought.

"What would you do if you did come home for good?" she asked out of real curiosity and because she was being Daisy-like in wanting him to think about it. "What job would you take on the ranch?"

He shrugged and shook his head. "No clue. Noah runs the place and quite well. His wife, Sara, is the forewoman. Daisy is in charge of all things guest. Axel's the safety guy and plans and leads wilderness tours, and his wife, Sadie, handles nutrition for the guests and staff. I guess I could be a cowboy. I wanted to be a cowboy when I was a kid."

Maisey smiled. "You're so good with children, maybe you could create some kind of educational program. I've been thinking along those lines of how to incorporate my ideas into the petting zoo and riding and the wilderness tours. We could have an entire program just for kids about ranch life. There's some of that already—Daisy gives great talks about the animals when she ventures into the petting zoo while guests are there."

He laughed. "Sounds like you've got that covered, Maisey. Maybe you could expand your role at the ranch. Director of Children's Programming, including running the Kid Zone and the educational activities."

"Me? Director?" She couldn't help but laugh. "I'm just a babysitter, Rex."

"There's no 'just' anything, Maisey. Caring for children is a huge responsibility. I'm just saying that your ideas are really great. You should work up a plan and talk to Daisy."

Huh. "You think so?"

"I absolutely do."

Maisey could barely contain her smile. "Maybe I'll wait a bit, though. It's my first week!"

"My motto? No time like now."

"Well, I appreciate the vote of confidence. I never would have thought of approaching my boss with ideas for children's programming."

He nodded at her with such reverence that her knees went a little weak. Had anyone ever made her feel like Rex did? Like anything was possible?

Not everything is, she reminded herself.

"Well, I'd better get started working on the

stage. I've got a design plan, and I'll get Axel or Noah to help me with the actual building of it."

Don't go. Stay right beside me and talk to me forever. Looking just the way you do. Looking at me just the way you do.

Boy, was she sunk with this guy.

"Oh—I meant to tell you," he said. "There's a Christmas shop in Prairie City that's open till nine every night till the big day. I thought we could go tonight after you close up and we can get whatever you need for the show, from an artificial tree or the trimmings to candy canes or a Santa suit. They have all kinds of Christmas costumes, too—elves, reindeer with red roses."

"Santa!" Maisey said. "I completely forgot that we'll need a Santa for the show. Can I sign you up?"

His gorgeous blue eyes went wide. "Did I just walk right into that?"

She laughed. "Yup. Sorry."

He shook his head with a smile. "My brothers will never let me live it down."

"I'll take that as a yes."

He grinned. "Ho, ho, ho. How was that?"

"Not bad." *Not bad at all, Rex Dawson. Too good, actually. You are* too *good. Which does make you too bad for me.*

"You make a list of what you need," he said,

"and we'll get everything tonight—the ranch will take care of the bill via your expense account, so go crazy." He tilted his head and looked at her. "If you're free to go, I mean."

What plans would she have? Singing the show songs to Chloe to get herself more and more used to hearing them. Avoiding the beautifully decorated tree in her living room, the one that Rex was responsible for. She loved the tree and it made her equally unsettled and sad. She kept telling herself that the tree, the holiday music, working on this show was all for Chloe, and it helped keep her thoughts focused on the now—not the past.

"Tonight would be great," she said. Going to the holiday shop—and she knew the one he meant—with a long list and no worries about price felt like a Christmas gift in itself. She'd never had an expense account before; she certainly wasn't used to being able to get the things she wanted so easily. "I'd love to have a bag of gifts for each child, just something small but personalized to hand out after the show. Maybe you can help me choose those, too. Like little plastic snow globes for the Caletti twins. They love the one of Santa's workshop on the front desk."

"I just got good at baby and toddler presents," he said. "I have no idea about big-kid gifts."

"What would you get Tyler the hoop star?" she asked, raising an eyebrow.

"Maybe a pair of neon laces for his sneakers and a Lakers cap."

Maisey grinned. "Exactly. You know more than you think about kids."

He raised an eyebrow. "Huh. I surprise myself sometimes."

Well, that was promising, Maisey thought—until she remembered she didn't put any stock in things turning around or changing. Things were what they were. Especially when the man in question put it right out there.

Leaving the day after Christmas. Not interested in fatherhood...

"Kiss, kiss, kiss, kiss!"

Maisey whirled around to see the kids all grinning and chanting at them.

Annalise stood on a chair behind them, holding up a sprig of mistletoe. Drat.

"Why do we never hear you sneak up on us?" Maisey asked, shaking her head with a smile.

"Stealth," Annalise said. "Kiss, kiss, kiss!"

Maisey rolled her eyes and stuck out her left cheek. Rex gave her a smooch to cheering and clapping.

"I'll, uh, just head over to where I'm gonna build the stage. Cupid, I need your help," he said to Annalise. "And, Tyler, you, too. You can be my construction assistants."

"Awesome," Tyler said, practically floating over beside Annalise.

Rex looked over his shoulder at her. "See you later, Maisey."

She honestly could not wait. But then, one day, she *wouldn't* see him later. She had to remember that.

Rex finally relaxed behind the wheel of his SUV as he turned onto the freeway, cars whizzing by. He'd been hyperaware of Maisey in the passenger seat. She smelled so good, which seemed impossible given that she'd been scrubbing glitter off her arms and one cheek when he'd arrived to pick her up. She'd also been glowing. The woman loved her job—and clearly was enjoying working on the Christmas show. She was definitely getting her Christmas spirit back.

She glanced behind her into the back seat, then bit her lip. "I keep forgetting that Chloe isn't with us. Sure was nice of Daisy to offer to watch her till we're back. First an expense report and now my own babysitter?"

Daisy had happened to pop into the Kid Zone to check on how things were going with the show when Rex had arrived to pick up Maisey, fully expecting to bring baby Chloe along on the trip to Prairie City. But when Daisy heard they were planning to do their shopping tonight, she'd offered to watch Chloe, loving the idea of Tony having a similar-aged little buddy for a few hours. The knowing looks his sister had sent him hadn't escaped his attention, either. She'd been clearly thrilled to give Rex and Maisey a few hours to themselves. Daisy the Matchmaker.

He mentally shook his head. "Well, like you said, Daisy has been trying to get me settled down back on the ranch. Putting us together in Prairie City is right up her alley. I'm surprised *she* didn't rush us with mistletoe."

She laughed. "I was thinking that myself."

Which meant his sister had been chatty with Maisey about how single Rex was.

He could feel her gaze on him. What was she thinking? Probably that they weren't a pair, anyway, even if he *were* the marrying and dad kind who had the type of job that could keep him nearby, home for dinner every night. She was so young, just twenty-three. And he was eight years older and world-weary and jaded.

Even still, Maisey felt like a part of him—she had ever since he'd found that bottle with her letter inside. He had to remember what was really driving him: his protectiveness toward her, the deep need to give her back Christmas. He wanted Maisey to have the world. That meant backing off from even thinking of acting on his attraction to her. Not easy, though. Another peck on the cheek, this one in the Kid Zone earlier today, had sent chills racing up all his nerve endings.

He could just imagine what a long, sexy, hot kiss on the lips, her body pressed against his, would do to him.

Get off the subject, he told himself. *She's not going to be yours. She needs someone who'll actually be around—very literally there for her.*

He cleared his throat. "I'm sure finding a great dad for Chloe is important to you. Daisy really is a serious matchmaker. Talk to her and you'll have five candidates lined up outside the Kid Zone."

He'd said it himself, the words had come out of his own mouth, but he felt a little bit sick because of it. *You're jealous, dope. You want her and can't have her, also at your own doing. So stop mooning over her like Tyler the dribble king does over Annalise.* The poor kid had almost dropped a heavy metal tape measure on his foot while they'd been working on how large to make the stage because he was deeply listening to Annalise talk about her favorite annual Christmas TV special—*Frosty the Snowman*.

This time he didn't feel Maisey looking at him.

He glanced over at her; she was staring out the window, kind of...glumly.

"I don't know," she said. "I do want Chloe to have a father. A great father. But I'm hardly ready to date, let alone to get serious about anyone. I can't even imagine trusting a guy."

"When you find the right person, all that will fall into place. He'll be right, feel right, and you'll find yourself trusting without even realizing it."

"I doubt I could be that carefree again. I got sweet-talked and lied to so many times by my ex. Right now I need to work on being independent. Socking enough savings away so that I have an emergency fund. Starting a college account for Chloe. That would mean the world to me. I'm not sure I'll ever get to college myself, but I'd like her to have the option, you know?"

He nodded. "I went to a state school on minimal loans and working part-time. I wouldn't have minded a big nest egg just for my education, but it just didn't exist. It feels good to make things happen for yourself. Like with what you want to do for yourself. If you want to go to college, you'll get there."

"I've been dreaming of getting a teaching degree forever. Trust me, I'm used to not getting what I want most."

He glanced at her, her cheeks so red that he

quickly turned his attention to the road to give her privacy.

"I hate that I said that. I'm not a whiner."

"What you are is incredible, Maisey. That's all you need to know."

She laughed. "You just feel bad for me." He looked over at her and her smile had faded. "I also hate that. Don't feel bad for me."

"Never said I did. And I don't. I think you've been through some really big stuff, Maisey Clark. And I think you're amazing because of what I've seen in the short time I've known you. That okay with you?"

The smile was back. "Yes. It is."

He laughed. "Good. That's settled, then. And here we are," he added. "Prairie City."

As he pulled into a diagonal spot in front of a coffee shop, she glanced around the bustling downtown. "I love and hate this town. The last foster home I was in was right up there." She pointed to a corner. Leaf Road. "I left the day I turned eighteen with a hug from the foster mom and my social worker, and that was that. Aged out and on my own with nothing."

"Want to show me the house?" he asked.

She bit her lip and shrugged. "I don't know. Maybe seeing it will give me closure on it."

"It might," he ventured.

She wrapped her arm around his, and he was so surprised that his knees kind of shook. Unless he was mistaken, and he didn't think he was, the gesture said *I trust you.* After all, she'd opened up in the car earlier; she did trust him. Certainly enough to show him the home, to have him beside her. To share her history.

He couldn't mess that up. He could not, under any circumstances, do anything to hurt that trust. It was precious and he knew it.

"Let's go, then," she said with something of a smile.

Let's go echoed in his head, all the various contexts and meanings. Every step he took with this woman led somewhere he'd never expected to be.

She looked so nervous about how she might feel about this trip down memory lane that he laid a hand on her arm. "I'm here for you," he said. "Okay?"

"I know you are."

Forget about ending up where he'd never expected. This was territory he'd never been in and had no idea how to navigate.

Chapter Seven

Standing across the street from the house, Maisey pulled her wool hat down low, not wanting the foster home mother to recognize her if she happened to look out the window or come outside. The woman had been nice enough, but first of all, Maisey knew how incredibly busy she was with the kids—seven during Maisey's time—and second, seeing her would just be too much.

Maisey had spent from ages sixteen to eighteen here, earning money by babysitting the younger kids when she was needed, and that was a big help in discovering how much she loved taking care of children. She'd help a couple of the kids with their schoolwork, particularly areas they struggled in, and Maisey found herself as a volunteer tutor, which was how she'd learned she'd wanted to be a teacher.

She stared up at the second-floor window, the farthest one to the left, barely feeling the cold snap of December air on her face. How many times had she sat by that window, just staring out and dreaming of "someday" and that things would be different?

"You okay?" Rex asked. He stood beside her, her arm still firmly wrapped around his.

"Actually, yes. I thought it would hurt seeing this place again since I always avoided this corner, let alone ever ventured down the street to anywhere near the house. But it turns out I discovered my passion here." She told him about babysitting and tutoring the kids. "I'll never forget when one girl I worked with came home from school with her first A ever. I was so proud of both of us." She smiled, remembering Bree's dark braid swishing around as she danced around their bedroom, waving the graded essay.

"Sometimes I think about adopting a child from foster care one day. Does that sound crazy? Too much on my plate as a single mother?"

"I think you could do anything you set your heart to, Maisey."

She felt herself beam. She'd heard people say that kind of thing before, but it had always sounded like a platitude. Coming from Rex, she believed it.

"And we already know you're a great mom," he continued. "I can just imagine what you could bring to a child in a position like you'd been in. You could change a life."

She was so touched she almost gasped. Instead, she wrapped her arms around him and kissed him, full on the lips.

"Oh," she whispered, not stepping back out of the embrace—though she'd meant to. Her brain had planned on it but her feet wouldn't move.

He leaned in and kissed her back. On the lips. Warm and strong and lingering long enough to let her know this was not a mistletoe kiss with kids watching. This was the real thing.

"I'm not supposed to kiss you," he said—and he did step back. "I'm gonna be honest, Maisey. I'm very attracted to you. On so many levels. But I am leaving the day after Christmas. That's set in stone."

"Is it?" she asked before she could stop herself. Maybe if he said yes, it was, she'd stop the back-and-forth on the subject of letting herself explore her feelings for him.

"Yes. Set in stone. I live on the road. My job is

across the entire country. That's who I am, who I've always been."

She raised an eyebrow. "I don't know about that. I've been learning that *I* direct my path, that my past doesn't get to dictate anything. Life changes. Things happen. We both know that. Paths twist and turn. Who says you have to stay on the same one?"

She could forget about giving up the back-and-forth.

He didn't respond for a few seconds. "We'd better get to Christmasland since the list is so long and the store closes at nine."

"It's barely seven," she pointed out. But she got it. He needed to move on. From her. And their conversation.

Not quite yet, sorry.

"So, if I fell in love with you, I'd be an idiot," she said. "That's not a question. Just something you should confirm."

He held her gaze, his blue eyes tender. "You're very smart, Maisey."

Disappointment hit her hard in the stomach, in the chest, in the region of where her heart was. "Got it," she said. "Do not fall in love with this guy. Leaving set in stone. Life on the road."

This time he didn't respond at all. He looked so

uncomfortable that she felt kind of bad for poking at him. But better they got this out in the open.

She knew now, for absolute sure. Because he said so.

Don't listen to Rex, she could hear Daisy Dawson McCord say if she told her about this conversation. *Two of my brothers said the same dumb thing about not being this or being that, and look at them now. Husbands. Fathers. And very happy.*

Luck had never been on Maisey's side, though.

She took one last look at the house where she'd spent two years worrying what life on the outside would be like. Maisey certainly hadn't been expected back for visits once she turned eighteen and had been nicely shown the door. There had been no invitations to Thanksgiving dinner or Christmas. *No wonder I wanted to get married so bad and so fast*, she thought. And then Thanksgiving and Christmas had still been big busts, hardly festive.

"Despite finding my path here, I remember feeling so powerless over my own life at the same time. Does that make sense?"

He nodded. "You weren't in charge of your own life. You were a minor. Back then, as kids, as teenagers, things weren't really in our control. Like my dad's drinking. All I wanted back then was to leave and never come back. Even though I spent half the time at my mom's with my brothers, the hard parts with my dad were the times that were most stamped on me. It's hard to let go of that stuff."

"I know what you mean."

He nodded kind of soberly, but with such emotion in his eyes, in his face, that she wanted to wrap her arms around him again.

"All I know is that, like you said, you're in charge of your own life now, Maisey. Adopting a child from foster care, becoming a teacher, running the children's programming at the ranch—all that you can make happen."

So why can't you give up on your life on the road and come home? she wanted to ask. *You're in charge, right?*

Actually, she knew why. She just didn't like the answer.

Because he doesn't really want to. That had to be why.

Christmasland was a huge party supply store that changed with the seasons or holidays. Over the summer it was a back-to-school center, then Halloween central, now Christmas. Rex had been in Christmasland a few times before, back when he was a kid with his father and stepmother, Leah—Noah and Daisy's mother. Rex, Axel and Zeke had been invited to go, as had Ford. Rex had probably come here with his parents when they were together, but he'd been too young to remember. Noah and Daisy's mother had wanted her stepsons to feel included in their Christmas at the ranch. The last time they'd all trooped over, their dad had taken out his credit card to pay the bill, but the card had been declined and Leah had said she was budgeted to the penny and they'd just have to forgo the tree that year, that Christmas was in their hearts, anyway. When Rex's mother had divorced their dad, she'd packed up all the Christmas stuff and taken it to their new apartment. So there was nothing in boxes in the attic—their dad had long sold off anything of their grandparents' that could bring in money for his gambling habit.

"I have forty-seven dollars from my paper route," Ford had said at the checkout, taking out his wallet and the cash.

Rex would never forget that. Their stepmother had started crying, which Rex hadn't understood at the time, and Bo Dawson had stormed out, embarrassed and angry. Leah had thanked Ford and told him to put the money back in his wallet, that the gesture was loving and generous but it was his money, and she'd repeated that "Christmas was in their hearts" and they didn't need all this stuff, anyway, right?

Rex had blocked out a lot of that time or maybe he'd just been too young to remember, but he'd never forget the little red Hot Wheels car he'd found wrapped with his name on it on the coffee table in the living room when he and his brothers had been dropped off on December 26 for "Christmas with Daddy." He'd overheard Bo and Leah arguing that it was awful that Ford had had to buy his brothers their presents from his father or else they'd have nothing.

Rex still had that Hot Wheels car. In fact, it lived in the front pocket of his carry-on bag, always there. Sometimes he'd dig around for a pack of tissues or gum and his fingers would land on the little car. Always made him smile. Every time that happened, he'd text Ford a hello out of the clear blue sky.

They'd never had a Christmas like that again at their dad's; Leah had apparently discovered that Bo Dawson lied about a lot of things and she budgeted to make sure their Christmas, for all the Dawson kids, was as it should be. When she'd passed away from cancer, Christmas at Dad's on the twenty-sixth had gone back to the old way. For Noah and Daisy, Christmas at Dad's was on the twenty-fifth and they'd learned to make their own holiday from Ford.

Regardless of all that, Christmas was special

but still something Rex had compartmentalized a long time ago as something not to get excited about. He couldn't remember the last time he really cared about Christmas. Because his father had died last December, all the siblings had gathered for the holiday at the then-broken-down ranch since they'd been scattered across Wyoming, Daisy's farmhouse barely standing then. His sister had said that Christmas was so big, so beautiful, that it should loom larger than their complicated grief and their dilapidated surroundings. But it hadn't, for any of them.

Now, as he stood in the brightly lit Christmasland, "White Christmas" playing over the loudspeaker, he wondered just what made him think he could help Maisey Clark get back her Christmas spirit when he had none himself.

"You okay?" she asked, eyeing him.

"Just thinking about Christmas past," he said. "Some whopper memories." He mock-shivered and attempted a smile.

She rubbed his arm. "I appreciate you taking me here, then, Rex. Christmas isn't the easiest for either of us, huh?"

"I always think I should be over childhood stuff, but then a memory floats into my head and pokes at the sore spots when I least expect it."

"Oh, trust me, I know. I just keep thinking

that everything I do, including being here, is for Chloe. New traditions. I think of her beautiful tiny face, her big hazel eyes, with the entire future in them, and everything needs to be about her, not me."

Same for me with you, he wanted to say. *That's what you bring out in me. You take me outside myself.*

Whoa. There it was again, the mystifying deep hold this woman had on him.

He glanced around to shake off his thoughts and get back on track. "Wow. Have you ever seen so many ornaments in your life?" He pointed at the section called Ornament Village off to the left. "Maybe we can find your Siamese cat."

He *had* to find that cat. Had. To. Hanging that replica on her Christmas tree would be the final clincher, the embodiment of Christmas restored.

She glanced over, not looking hopeful at all. "Maybe, but I doubt it. I looked on Christmasland's website many times, but they never had it. Other cat ornaments, yes, but not the one I'd had in my hand when my dad rescued me from the house."

This time he did shiver. And everything he felt about Maisey Clark was reinforced. She deserved the world.

"Did you have a Siamese cat? Was that the significance of that ornament in the first place?"

Oh, God. Why had he asked that? If she'd lost the cat in the fire, too, his brain would explode.

She shook her head. "My dad was so allergic, but Siamese cats were my mom's favorite. She loved their slinky beauty. My mom told me that when my dad surprised her with the ornament and hung it on the tree, he'd said it was kinda like giving her a Siamese cat for Christmas every year."

He smiled. "That's really nice."

Her smile lit up her face. "Yeah. They really loved each other. I don't remember much about them but I do remember feeling that, knowing that. I guess it's why I'm still something of a romantic."

"You probably like this song, then," he said as Nat King Cole filled their ears.

She grinned and bowed and held out her hand, and he smiled and gave her a twirl, coming to a stop so close against him he could barely handle it.

"Well," she said, stepping away a bit. "We'd better hit the aisles." She pulled out her list from her tote bag. "Let's start with your Santa suit. Gotta have that."

Rex wasn't much of a dancer, but he did like slow dancing. And that one twirl to Nat King Cole had him imagining holding her close, chest to chest, her head on his shoulder, her arms around his neck, his around her waist. Never letting her go…

Two kids in Santa hats with furry white beards Velcroed around their heads went racing past, and he shook off the very pleasant, welcome thoughts about him and Maisey.

"You know, those whirlwinds who just ran past reminded me of something," he said. "I'm ninety-nine percent sure there's a Santa suit in the attic at Daisy's house. I was up there looking for something last time I was at the ranch, and I know I saw the outfit, if not the beard. I can check when we pick up Chloe tonight. If I'm imagining things, I can come back and buy one."

"Okay, annotating my list," she said, grabbing a pen from her bag and jotting that down. "One thing I am—organized. So let's get the kids' costumes. We need ten altogether and I've noted sizes and who's wearing what."

"You mean eleven," he said. "Chloe has to have a costume, too."

She stared at him, a slow, sweet smile on her lips. "You are so right. And thoughtful. You should stop it." She laughed, but he caught something in her expression—wistfulness, maybe? Which reminded him what she'd noted earlier. *If I fell in love with you, I'd be an idiot.*

Was she falling for him? How the hell could he give her a great Christmas if he'd let that happen and then walked away on the twenty-sixth? He'd leave her with a broken heart.

He hadn't figured that in. Rex hadn't allowed himself to get close to a woman since he'd hurt Bethany six months ago. He cared so much about Maisey—no way was he setting her up like this.

Dammit to hell.

"Said too much?" she asked, her lips kind of twisted to one side.

"You said what needed to be said. I should back off, Maisey. We both know I'm leaving for my job."

"For you, you mean."

"No, for my job. For the US Marshals. For Joe, the witness out there somewhere. For all the witnesses, all the victims, their families. What I do is important."

"I know it is, Rex. I didn't mean that it wasn't."

"Let's shop," he said. "That's what we're here for, right?"

She looked down, her expression full-out crestfallen, and he wanted to kick himself in the stomach. "Yeah. Let's shop. Okay," she said, eyes on her list. "Reindeer suit size 3T for Danny Daw-son."

He closed his eyes for a second, inwardly sigh-ing as his adorable nephew's face came to mind. Danny would go crazy over his reindeer suit. He would absolutely love it. And Rex would have to say goodbye the day after Christmas when the two of them were getting so close.

"Right. Reindeer suit size 3T. I'm on it."

As they headed to the costume area, Maisey grabbed a bright green elf hat with pointy felt ears sticking out on either side and put it on her head. "How do I look?" she asked with a grin.

"You look really beautiful," he said—too seri-ously, too reverently. But she did.

Somehow, he'd just have to stop looking at her and thinking about her.

Chapter Eight

Rex stood with Maisey at the checkout, noticing her eyes widen at the grand total of their shopping spree.

"That's more than a month's rent at my old trailer," she said.

He handed over his credit card, that old memory of his father's being declined making him grateful every time he purchased something. "The ranch is doing really well since the grand reopening last summer, and we all want to make the kids' show unforgettable. And trust me, the reason Daisy didn't join you on this mission is because she would have gone way overboard, every bell and whistle."

"I am looking forward to seeing the kids' faces when we hand out costumes for the rehearsals."

"Same here," he said, surprising himself, but it was true. Even just spending a bunch of hours working on the set, he'd gotten to know Tyler and Annalise pretty well just by listening to them talk, how they responded. The Kid Zone bunch were great kids.

"I'm trying to convince my special song apprentice—Zara—to be in the show, but so far she refuses. I think she'll change her mind once she sees her elf costume. I found one with purple felt shoes and purple stripes on the pointy hat, and purple is her favorite color."

"They're really lucky to have you, Maisey. It's obvious how much you care about them and your job."

"Good, because I do care. But I feel like the lucky one. Having the job in the first place, meeting such wonderful people, like this family called the Dawsons." She smiled. "Seriously, all of you are so generous. I know you have issues with your dad, Rex, but in between the hard times, he must have done something right. Then again, maybe your moms were just one thousand percent superstars. Probably, now that I think about it more."

"We did get lucky with great moms. All of us. My dad had great taste in wives." He pictured his mom down in her Florida backyard, cutting into an orange from her own little grove. He'd have to plan a trip down soon. "But you're also right. In between, even far and few, he got things right. He cared about us. We know that. It took me a long time to see it, to believe it, but I understand more about addiction than I once did."

She squeezed his hand and he didn't want her to let go.

"I don't know about you, but I'm starving," he said. "Want to grab some dinner?"

There—nice and casual. Rex could actually go for a filet mignon with peppercorns and roast potatoes, but he wasn't sure he should suggest a real restaurant—à la what would feel like a date.

"Definitely," she said as she took two bags, one dangling from each wrist, and he took the rest. "I need to replenish my energy. Remember, I'm not used to shopping and buying everything my heart desires. Every kid has a holiday costume. The show gets its own Christmas tree. Each song has its own fun prop. I still can't believe it."

"The show would be special with just the kids singing. But Daisy wants to go to town for our guests during Christmas, so might as well go big."

They headed out to his SUV and loaded the cargo space. Then he glanced around at the restaurants lining the main street, looking in the windows for well-lit, no-candles-in-the-center tables.

"You know what I'm so in the mood for right now?" she asked. "A great pizza. With spinach and mushrooms and peppers."

He instantly relaxed. "Can my half have meatball and sausage?"

"Definitely. And garlic knots on the side."

Maisey knew of a small pizzeria that had been in business for decades and had always been her favorite, so they went there. Loud and very brightly lit, the pizza joint was probably the least romantic restaurant in town. But as they sat at their square table and shared their extra-large pie with their favorite toppings and their basket of garlic knots, Rex felt like he was on one of the best dates of his life. Easy, fun, natural. No awkward silences.

Because it's not a date. You and Maisey even covered the two of you earlier. There is no "the two of you." You're leaving and she needs permanence. End of story.

With two slices of veggie wrapped up for Maisey to take home—Rex had demolished his half—they finally got back in the SUV and headed home to the ranch.

Home to the ranch. It was Maisey's home now—not his.

Interesting.

On the way back, they talked about the show and the costumes and whether one day, fifteen years from now, they'd hear that Tyler and Annalise were engaged. Once again, their conversation was so effortless and rich. There was no small talk, nor did they get heavy and deep as they had earlier.

If I fell in love with you, I'd be an idiot...

He'd tried over the past couple of hours to stop thinking about that, but her words had kept popping back into his brain.

As they arrived at Daisy's farmhouse so Maisey could pick up Chloe, he thought about how she'd hugged him in front of the foster home. How she'd held his arm. The way she'd looked at him in Pauletta's Pizza.

The way he'd been unable to take his eyes off her.

They'd already fallen for each other, he knew. And both of them would be smart and not act on it.

"I can't wait to see Chloe," Maisey said, taking off her seat belt. "I miss her so much. I never feel quite right when I'm away from her. Like something is missing."

That's how I've felt since I met you, he almost said, and thank God he didn't. *Whoa.*

How had this woman come to mean so much to him so fast? The combination of the Dear Santa letter, her old dream not coming true, finding out she was a single mother totally on her own again and his wild reaction to her physically, emotionally, mentally. He couldn't spend long with his rogue thoughts because Daisy had clearly heard the car and opened the front door with a grin.

"Chloe is the sweetest, prettiest little thing and so easy," his sister said as she held the door open wide for them. "She and Tony stared at each other and waved their little arms at each other for a while. Then both conked out. They're fast asleep."

"Thanks so much for watching her," Maisey said. "We got everything on the list." She told Daisy about the costumes and the Kid Zone tree and the trimmings they'd gotten. "All that's left are the small gifts for the kids to go under the tree."

"Thanks for doing all that," Daisy said to both of them. "And if you two want to go present shopping after work tomorrow, I'd be thrilled to watch Chloe again."

Another night out with Maisey. Another shouldn't-be-romantic-but-it-will-be-anyway dinner. Another half-hour drive back to the ranch, talking, sharing, being so aware of her in such close proximity.

But they did need to get the kids' gifts. And he couldn't leave that to Maisey on her own since there were quite a few to buy. And he *had* gotten to know some of the children enough to really help out. Rationalizing was a great thing.

"Works for me," Rex said. "Pick you up at six, Maisey?" He only casually glanced at her, no big whoop here, just two…friends doing some Christmas shopping. And really, it was work related.

He felt her gaze on him, lingering before she responded.

"Sounds good," she said. "Six it is."

Daisy beamed. Of course. "Great. I'll swing by a bit earlier to pick up Chloe."

"That sure makes things easier for me," Maisey said. "Thanks. Oh, hey," she added to Rex. "Don't forget the Santa costume. You said there would probably be one up in the attic?"

"Oh, right." He looked at Daisy. "Seemed a waste to buy new at the everything's-marked-up Christmas shop tonight when I'm ninety percent sure there's one in the attic."

Daisy nodded. "There definitely is. In the back by that collection of junk Dad was trying to fix up to sell, I think. Everything up there was stuff he couldn't sell on Craigslist, and good thing— there's a few things I'm glad to have of our grandparents, even if they're very old and if dusty throw pillows live in the attic. I know they're there."

"It's surprising he didn't sell the suit," Rex pointed out. "Very few things had nostalgic value to Bo Dawson, but maybe Santa did."

Daisy nodded and shrugged. "Dad was a mystery."

"Since Chloe's sleeping," Maisey said, "I'd love to take a peek and see what old-timey gems might be hiding in plain sight. I love antiquing."

A kettle started whistling in the kitchen, and Daisy hurried toward it. "I'm about to make a mug of spiced lemon tea, if anyone's interested."

"Thanks, but I'm stuffed with pizza and soda," Rex said with a pat on his stomach.

"Me, too," Maisey added. "But thanks."

"Well, sounds like you two had a *very* productive evening," Daisy said with a grin as she disappeared into the kitchen.

Rex rolled his eyes with a smile. Standard Daisy, all right. "That narrow door in the hallway opens to stairs that go up to the attic." As in the SUV earlier, he was so aware of Maisey beside him as he headed over and opened the door, flicking on the light switch. He hadn't been up here in a long, long time.

"What are those?" Maisey asked when they were at the landing, pointing at the six identical trunks with name labels lined up single file against the back wall.

"My grandparents bought one for each of us when we were born," he said. "There's not much in each. Some baby stuff, kid art, class pictures, the usual."

"Show me something in your trunk," she said.

"You want to see a school picture of my awkward stage at twelve?" he asked. "You'll go running out of the attic."

"No way did you ever have an awkward stage. You're too good-looking. And don't let that go to your head."

"Too late," he said, shooting her a grin. He walked over to the trunk and opened the lid, looking at some old clothes he was surprised his dad hadn't tried to sell, then realized why Bo hadn't. He stood completely still, staring at the brown-and-gold Wyoming Cowboys football T-shirt his brother Ford had given him for his thirteenth birthday. He'd been wearing that T-shirt for good luck under a sweater on his very first date when he was fifteen. The date had been a total disaster. He'd taken the girl to a burger place that now was no longer around, and she'd actually managed to get back together with her ex-boyfriend, a jock whom Rex couldn't stand, right on the date. The reunited couple had actually left together, leaving Rex sitting there with both their untouched plates, which hadn't even been served when his date had abandoned him. Rex had called home for a ride, hoping Ford would be around since it was the weekend, but he wasn't, and his dad had shown up. Bo had come inside the burger joint, and Rex had told him the basic gist, feeling like a total loser.

Bo had sat down, said there was no reason the girl's perfectly good cheeseburger should go to waste and took a big bite, then gobbled up a few fries. Rex had found that both mortifying and hilarious, and his dad told him stories about his own dating days back at Bear Ridge Middle School. They'd talked for a good hour, Rex laughing his head off, and his chest had been bursting with love for his dad. That night, Bo Dawson had gotten drunk and passed out outside, something he often did, and Rex and his brothers, visiting for the weekend, couldn't budge him. They'd had to cover him with a down blanket and leave him on the patio. Half of Rex's goodwill toward his father from earlier that night had been replaced by the usual dread. Complicated.

His lucky T-shirt hadn't seemed so lucky given all that had happened, and Rex had tossed it in the trash in a fit of teenage angst, but apparently his dad had fished it out and washed it and saved it. Because here it was.

"When's the last time you poked around your trunk?" Maisey asked.

He shrugged. "This is the first time. I asked Daisy what was in the trunks and she said old clothes, school photos, nothing of interest. And if Daisy says nothing of interest, there's *really* nothing to see, since she tends to make a big fuss of little stuff."

Maisey smiled. "I'm like that, too."

He glanced around, hoping to find something with a lock that the key his dad left him would look like it fit. There was nothing. What did the key open? Maybe he'd never find out. He'd had an entire year, ever since finding the key in the otherwise empty envelope with his name on it in his dad's scrawled handwriting, to think long and hard about what his dad could have wanted him to find, to open. He still had no idea. At first he'd focused on the personal—what hidden meaning was there? But the less he found a lock the key opened, the more he just looked for any lock to try. He was out of locks.

Frustrated, he opened a box near his dad's collection of broken small electronics and there was the Santa suit—even the beard was there, smushed into the sleeve.

"Success," he said, pulling it out and holding it up. He put on the hat.

Maisey grinned. "Back in Christmasland, I felt like you were my own Santa. Now you truly look the part."

"That's exactly who I'm supposed to be for you." He gave a firm nod, reminded of his purpose in her life. Not to kiss her or fall for her. To be her Santa, to restore her Christmas spirit, to give her the holiday she deserved.

A baby's cry could be heard downstairs.

"That's definitely Chloe," Maisey said. "I can't wait to see her sweet little face. I haven't been away from her this long before."

Rex closed his trunk and tucked the Santa suit firmly under his arm. "I'll get you two home."

But again, he didn't want their night to come to an end.

"I just realized something," Rex said as he carried the last of the bags into Maisey's cabin while she settled Chloe in her high chair in the kitchen.

Maisey poked her head out from the kitchen doorway. "What's that?"

He held out the Santa suit. "I'd better see if this thing fits now before I find out it's three sizes too small on the day of the show."

"Bathroom's right there. It's pretty small, so

don't try to turn around once you get the padded top part of the suit on."

He smiled. "Thanks for the warning."

She sat down beside Chloe's high chair, which she'd just started using a week ago, and dipped the little spoon into her daughter's favorite dinner, butternut squash baby food. Chloe had gotten through half the jar when a "Ho, ho, ho" could be heard in the hallway.

Santa appeared in the doorway of the kitchen, his hands on his hips. "Fits just right. Christmas is saved."

It certainly is, she thought. "All you need is a bag of gifts slung over your shoulder."

"Ah, speaking of that. Maybe we should make a list of what you want to get the kids so that when we hit the stores tomorrow night, we already have the hard part figured out."

"Good idea. By the time you're done changing out of that thing, Chloe will have finished her dinner, so I'll meet you on the sofa. I have half a pie that Cowboy Joe gave me to take home from the cafeteria. Want some and coffee?"

"Definitely," he said before heading toward the bathroom again.

"I like him too much," she whispered to her baby girl.

Chloe's big hazel eyes focused on her, a little smile on her face.

"You like him, too. I can tell. He's pretty wonderful."

"Meow," Snowbell said, slinking between the legs of the chair, and Maisey took that to mean she also liked Rex Dawson. Everyone did, it seemed.

But some people, like herself, had to watch out from liking him too much, even though she was clearly past that point.

She finished feeding Chloe, lifting the baby from the high chair against her chest and giving her some good pats for a burp. Success.

"How about some tummy time?" she asked Chloe. "On your favorite mat." She carried Chloe into the living room and set her on the thick mat with lots to touch and look at. Chloe gurgled and lifted her head, batting at a low-hanging pompom from a spiral felt stick.

The bathroom door opened and all six feet two inches of Rex, back in his sexy Henley shirt and jeans, was headed toward her, his hair slightly mussed from the hat.

"I bought my niece and nephews a mat just like that," he said. "Turns out Noah and Daisy both had gotten at least four as gifts. Thanks to having baby relatives, I even know what Chloe is doing is called tummy time."

Maisey laughed. "You're an involved uncle. I love that."

"I surprisingly do, too," he said, sitting down. He glanced at the coffee table. "Hey, where's that pie you promised me? I'm surprised I have room for anything more after all that pizza, but I do," he added, patting his rock-hard stomach. Not that Maisey knew for sure it was, but she could imagine through the thin cotton shirt.

"Oh, right!" she said, popping up.

"Nope, you sit and relax. I'll get it and make the coffee."

Of course he would. He was like that.

"Decaf or regular?" he called from the kitchen.

"Definitely decaf," she said. "With cream and a sugar cube from the yellow bowl on the table."

"Coming right up, madame."

Maisey smiled and leaned close to Chloe's ear. "I could seriously get used to this."

Her ex-husband had never made a pot of coffee or said anything remotely like "Coming right up, madame," let alone told her to sit and relax. She'd thought she'd wanted a traditional guy so that she could be "wifely," but that had gotten old fast. Her ex had just wanted to be waited on, picked up after and catered to, in all departments. If Maisey ever got married again, she'd have a real partner who reciprocated, shared in the household duties, rubbed her feet after she gave an excellent back massage. She might not have had a good marriage, but at least she knew what she didn't want in a husband.

Rex came into the living room with a tray holding two slices of pecan pie and two mugs of coffee, which he set on the coffee table. Maisey scooped up Chloe and gave her a kiss and settled her in her baby swing, her alert eyes following her mother's every move.

Maisey sat on the sofa, Rex just a foot away beside her, and she got out her phone to start the list of gifts in her Notes app. They started in alphabetical order. The As alone took a good fifteen minutes since there were the twins, Amelia and Ava, and Annalise. If Maisey blanked on a good idea for someone, Rex came up with just the right present. They were a solid team.

Solid team. More and more, Maisey couldn't deny just how deep her feelings for him went. Or that if anyone asked her what she wanted for Christmas, it would be for Rex to stay.

Luckily, she couldn't focus on him or wonder what a lasting kiss would feel like because they were moving right along on their mission. By the time their refills of coffee and all the pie was gone, the gift list was practically done and full of everything from art supplies to bug-catching kits to stuffed animals. There was only one name left: Zara.

"Hmm," Maisey said. "I want to get this exactly right. Zara opened up to me earlier today. She's been through a lot."

"Long dark hair? The song apprentice, right? Maybe something related to music or a streaming gift card?"

"Something personal, though." She took a sip of her coffee, hoping the perfect idea would come to her.

"The other day, when I was in the Bear Ridge gift shop, I saw something on a display by the counter that might work. A silver musical note pin, and the store was offering free engraving for Christmas for all the jewelry."

Maisey gasped. "Rex Dawson, how the hell do you do it?"

He tilted his head. "Do what?"

"Come up with the perfect everything?"

That got her a smile. "I just happened to notice the music pins because I was looking for something for my sisters-in-law in that shop."

"What did you get them?" she asked, deeply curious about everything concerning this man and his life.

"Nothing at the gift shop, so I asked for help from my bros. I got Sadie a ten-session class at new-mother yoga since she'll be delivering this spring, and I ended up getting Sara a ton of stuff for her garden bed—seeds Noah said she wanted and a bunch of big planting pots."

"Very thoughtful."

"I still have to get for two brothers—Ford and Zeke—they're the ones that don't live on the ranch, either. And Danny. Then I'm done with family gifts."

"I just have to buy a few. I haven't decided what I'm getting Chloe. I saw some adorable pink-and-purple polka-dot socks. And a couple new books. And I saw a teething toy in the shape of a moose that was so cute."

"I think Chloe will love all that." He finished the rest of his coffee. "Maisey, can I ask you something personal?"

She sat up straighter. "Do we talk about anything else?"

He smiled. "No, I guess not. We go straight for the heart of the matter. I was wondering if you got presents when you were a kid. At the group homes."

"The house parents always bought each kid something small. They tried to make it personal. One year when I really liked drawing, Miss Meredith got me a pack of pastels and a sketch pad. I loved that." She glanced at him. "You were picturing me giftless, weren't you? Not even a lump of coal."

"I hoped not. I just wondered."

"Tell me about a special Christmas gift you received," she said, again way too curious about all things Rex Dawson.

"My favorite Christmas present ever was a mountain bike—I rode that everywhere. And a little Matchbox car my oldest brother gave me one year."

"Hmm, I do think we have a theme—vehicles. Transportation. Movement."

He tilted his head and stared at her. "I never thought about that. But you're probably right. Does kinda represent me."

"You could have one of those buggies I've seen on the ranch. Like Daisy drives around in." Oh, no. Did she just say that? Would he think she was asking him to stay at the ranch? They'd already discussed that and he was leaving. He'd made that very clear.

Chloe let out a giant yawn.

Maisey scooped up her baby girl from the swing and gave her a snuggle. "I'd better get her to bed. Back in a jiff."

He looked at her but didn't say anything. She went into the nursery and changed Chloe, got her into fresh pj's and then settled the baby against her chest in the rocking chair. "How about a story, sweet girl?" Maisey grabbed the book that was on the table beside the chair. "We didn't finish this one about the bunny. But let's start from the beginning." She opened the book with one hand, the other caressing Chloe's back. "'Fluffers the bunny rabbit loves tomatoes. But he's the only rabbit in the whole village who does. All the other bunnies only love carrots.'"

She turned the page but Chloe's eyes were already closed. "Today was a big day. Kid Zone, then a playdate with your new friend Tony. Let's get you in your crib."

She carefully got up and laid Chloe down. Then she watched her baby sleep, her little chest with the penguins across it going up and down. When she turned to leave, Rex was standing in the doorway.

Please don't say you're leaving. I'm not ready for this night to end.

"You're such a good mother," he said. "Devoted, committed."

She smiled. "Go on."

He laughed, then put his hand over his mouth. "I don't want to wake her up," he whispered.

Before she could stop herself, she lifted on her tiptoes and kissed him. A real kiss. *Kiss me back,* she thought. *C'mon.*

He did. He put his hands on either side of her face and looked at her for a moment, then kissed her as if he'd been waiting to all night.

"I'd better go," he said. "Staying here for even one more second is dangerous."

She smiled but she hardly felt it anywhere inside. There was something so tender and beautiful between them, but he wasn't giving it a chance. She shouldn't, either. But just letting him go back to his old world, his old life, when he had this shiny new warm love in his life? Without fighting for what was happening between them?

Was he making love impossible for himself? Or did he just not love her?

Right now, that was the question she had to answer. No—*he* did.

Chapter Nine

The next morning, Noah and Axel stood on ladders on either side of the Dawson Family Guest Ranch Christmas Fair banner, waiting for Rex to determine if it was hanging straight. The fifteen-foot silver poles the banner hung from had been flanking the start of the path to the ranch, just past the gates, for fifty years, and though their dad had crashed into one pole drunk in a buggy one night, it was so sturdy it stayed put. Rex knew Noah had always thought that was a good omen for the ranch itself.

"Noah, up about an eighth of an inch and we're golden," Rex called.

The ranch was now all set for the festivities, a one-day extravaganza for the guests to stop at tables set up along the paths and in the lodge with holiday crafts to make and Christmas cookies to eat and eggnog and spiced cider to drink. Noah and Sara and their crew had decked out the ranch just enough so that it positively twinkled but still felt rustic. There would be stations set up in the Kid Zone to make ornaments and small gifts, free-flowing eggnog and spiced sugar cookies, and candy canes galore. And Rex would be playing Santa for the day in the red-and-green "hut" that he, Noah and Axel had built by the Christmas tree in the hallway of the lodge. He had no idea what that would be like, a lot of kids whispering in his ear about what they wanted for Christmas. What if they didn't get what they asked for? He'd feel terrible. Not that he'd know.

He still felt stung on Maisey's behalf, though. She hadn't gotten her Christmas wish and then had stopped making wishes altogether.

Noah and Axel climbed down, shaking him from his thoughts, and headed to the barn to put away the ladders. A silver pickup came up the asphalt path, which was weird since it was barely seven in the morning and cars weren't allowed on the drives past the gate. Rex squinted to see who it was in the bright morning sunshine.

The driver gave a short honk and stuck his head out the window. "Hey, stranger."

Rex grinned. His brother Ford. And was that Zeke in the passenger seat?

Ford parked by Daisy's house and he hopped out, followed by, yup, Zeke, just as Noah and Axel were coming back from the barn.

"I was talking to Zeke a couple nights ago and we both realized our Christmas vacations were starting this morning," Ford said when they approached, "so we decided to drive up together. We have way too many presents for everyone, especially the kids."

Rex hadn't seen these two brothers in a few months, but not a thing had changed—both still looked exactly like who they were. Ford, a cop, wore aviator sunglasses, had short dark hair and always seemed ready to help in any situation. Zeke, a businessman in mergers and acquisitions, might as well have been wearing a suit for how pristine his button-down shirt and dark jeans were, not a mark on his leather boots. All the Dawsons, particularly the brothers, looked like their father.

"What?" came the happy screech of Daisy Dawson McCord as she ran out the front door of the farmhouse. "It's a Christmas miracle! My five brothers are all home!" She threw her arms around Ford and Zeke, talking a mile a minute about the ranch and the fair. "Staying with us?" she asked them. "We've got room. Rex has been staying at Axel's, but now it's my turn. You guys have to stay at the farmhouse, too. It's my dream come true to have my brothers under one roof."

"Does Tony wake up all night long still?" Zeke asked with a grin. "With this mug, I need my beauty sleep."

"Now that he's five months, he actually sleeps through the night," Daisy said. "Well, till five thirty in the morning, anyway. But that's ranching hours, too, so I'll get your rooms ready with fresh linens." She ran toward the house. "Tony is going to be so happy all his uncles are here. Big dinner at the house tonight—so don't make any other plans!" She headed inside, the storm door closing behind her.

"Guess that's settled," Axel said. "My cabin will feel empty without you and River, Rex."

"River?" Ford asked, getting their bags from the back seat.

"My dog," Rex said. "Shepherd mix. Great guy. Supersmart, knows his commands, no aggression, major snuggler with a certain toddler named Danny Dawson."

"Wait," Ford said. "I'm still on the words *my*

dog coming out your mouth. *You* have a dog? You're here for good?"

Rex felt his smile fade. "No. I'm leaving the day after Christmas." He explained about finding River and taking him to the ranch. "Daisy takes care of River when I'm not around. Which will be a long stretch once I leave. I probably won't be back till…" He tried to think of upcoming holidays or special dates. "Ah—Danny's third birthday in March. I'll try to stay for a couple days."

"You'd better," Axel said. "Danny asks every morning at the crack of dawn when Unck Rex is going to wake up."

"He means that figuratively," Zeke said with a grin.

Rex gave him a playful jab in the side.

"Who's up for breakfast at the Bear Ridge Diner?" Ford asked. "Like old times." Last December, after they'd inherited the ranch, they'd spent a lot of time at that diner, holding family meetings since none of them could bear being on the dilapidated property for long.

"Sounds good. I'll go get Daisy," Rex said.

"I'll let Sara know we're skipping out," Noah said, grabbing his phone from his pocket.

He took the farmhouse porch steps two at a time, waved hello to his brother-in-law, Harrison, told his sister the plan, and of course she was thrilled. Daisy gave Harrison a kiss, handed him Tony and said she'd be back by nine.

Daisy practically skipped down the steps toward the car as the four other Dawsons piled in. "So…"

Rex eyed her. "So what?"

"How are things between you and Maisey?" She all but wiggled her eyebrows.

He mock-grimaced at her. "Things are *not.* Daisy, in all seriousness, don't play matchmaker when I'm leaving town in days."

"The matchmaking part is supposed to make you stay." She smiled but seemed wistful. "You have no idea what it means to me to see you all here at the same time. I'm selfish and want you all on the ranch for good. We're all we have, Rex. Come home."

There was a time when this line of talk from Daisy didn't poke at him—just Daisy being her usual loving, family-oriented self, and he'd always appreciated it since she'd long been the glue for the six of them, asking, bribing, to get them together. But now something was stabbing at him and it wasn't just Maisey and his crazy feelings for her. He'd been restless and stressed for months now, and coming home had calmed him— unexpectedly. But he belonged out on the road, hunting fugitives and helping witnesses. That was his mission in life.

He'd talk to Ford about it. As a cop, Ford would understand the grip the job had on him for many reasons.

Ford drove the half hour to town. The Bear Ridge Diner wasn't crowded, but there were hellos to say to the folks scattered at the counter and tables, including the chief of police at the Bear Ridge PD and one of his officers, both of whom kidded Noah about how they still couldn't believe he'd ever been a wild troublemaker as a teenager and young adult. Rex knew that, once, that kind of talk used to bother Noah, who'd completely changed his life when he'd taken on the rebuilding of the guest ranch. Now even Noah said he couldn't seem to remember himself as that "rowdy kid."

There was a big round table in the back of the diner, their waiter appearing with a coffee urn before he even handed out menus. They all nodded about the coffee, Daisy asking for decaf. Fifteen minutes later, once the plates of omelets and French toast and pancakes were served, the coffee refilled, the orange juice sipped, the siblings dug in, talking and laughing about themselves and the ranch.

"Hey, Ford," the chief of police said, winding his way toward them as he and the officer were leaving. "I know you're on the force out in Casper, but you should know we're going to have two openings after the New Year. One in January, one in March. I have two retiring, like O'Connor here." He clapped an arm on his officer's shoulder. "Think about it."

"I will, thank you," Ford said with a nod.

When the cops left, Daisy pounced. "How many people are offered a job without even asking for one? It's meant to be, Ford. We'll all help build your luxe log cabin on the ranch, and you can start your new job in January or April."

Ford took a sip of his coffee. "Maybe."

Rex almost choked on his bite of western omelet. "Did you just say *maybe*? I thought you said hell would ice over before you ever moved back to the ranch."

Ford took another slug of coffee. "That was last year. When everything the ranch used to be was still very fresh. Now it's hard to even remember those days. Every time I come visit I feel like I'm at the western version of Disney World. Well, not really, but you know what I mean. The place is *happy*."

Huh. Rex had to agree. All the old reasons for avoiding home no longer *were*.

"You'll seriously consider the offer?" Rex

asked his eldest brother as he forked a home fry. Casper was a city with close to 60,000 people. Bear Ridge barely had a population of 2,000.

Ford nodded. "Yeah, I think I will."

There was tension in his expression, despite the poker-face cop neutrality he was known for. Rex could see it. Something was driving him away from Casper. Relationship? Stress of the job? He really did need to talk to Ford in private.

"You could take the other opening," Ford said to Rex, eyeing him with the assessing gaze Rex was used to giving. "You were a cop for a year before you were accepted into the US Marshals' rigorous training program. Given all your experience, you can easily make detective."

"Someone pass the smelling salts," Daisy said. "I might have Ford and Rex moving home? Zeke, I'm still coming for you. But you're safe right now since I'll work on these two."

They all laughed, and the waiter came by to check on them, the question in the air about Rex joining the PD luckily lost in the chatter and then Axel telling a funny story about Danny.

But he could feel Ford's gaze on him, and he knew his brother could tell he was conflicted. Understatement. The call to leave—no commitments, no obligations, no emotional entanglements, no one relying on him except his boss and those he served—was strong, a force deep inside him. But as Maisey and her six-month-old came to mind, he felt the call to stay drumming like a tap in his heart.

At the Kid Zone, Chloe was screaming her head off and none of Maisey's usual tricks worked. Not holding the baby, rocking her, singing to her, burping her, carrying her vertically, horizontally or giving her swing time, which Chloe usually loved. Danny, Axel and Sadie's toddler, had his hands over his ears while sitting at a little table with his superhero coloring book. A few other kids kept looking over with frowns.

I know. Trust me, I know. I don't like the screeching, either. Her ace staffer, Hannah, was in the middle of a game with three kids, and the other sitter had called in sick. And now the Caletti twins were marching over, crying, too, faces furious, and each swiping at the other.

"No, you're the dumb one, dummy!" Ava yelled.

"You are, idiot!" Amelia screamed. "I'm telling Mom the minute she picks us up what you did!"

"Fine! I'm telling Dad!" Ava screeched back.

Maisey rocked and patted Chloe's back, praying the baby would calm down so that she could listen to the Calettis, who were marching closer, about to demand Maisey's attention, and boy, did they need it.

A question Maisey had asked during her job interview came roaring back into her mind. What if her attention was torn between guests' children and her own baby? She'd given an example of Chloe screaming, much like she was doing now, and a kid needing her attention, whether a bullying situation or a badly skinned knee, while the other staffers were busy with others. If she gave her attention to her baby because she'd need to address the crying, would that mean she was putting her own daughter first and not doing her job?

Daisy's answer had made her feel a lot better: *there is no yours or ours or theirs, Maisey.* Her boss had basically said that the kids in her care included guests, staff and Maisey's own, and that no one child deserved more or less attention than another because of who they were. *You have solid experience in knowing what takes priority,* Daisy had said, *and I trust you'll make good decisions.*

That response was soothing right now because quieting Chloe took priority so that everyone else could hear themselves think.

"Ho, ho, ho!" a deep voice called from the front door.

Rex Dawson entered in his sexy leather jacket and a Santa hat, lugging a large piece of wood, part of the backdrop that would appear onstage behind where the children would stand and sit. "Guess what, set apprentices," he called out. "It's backdrop painting time! Tyler, Annalise, that means you," he called out in a funny voice that went up and down and echoed.

Even the Caletti twins giggled.

Oh, Rex, bless you.

"And I need two more painting helpers," Rex said. "Ava, Amelia, how about you guys? You're master painters."

Their faces brightened immediately, but Maisey could see the girls were torn between telling on each other and getting to be on the painting crew with the teenagers, whom they seemed to look up to.

"Only if you're not annoying," Ava said, hands on hips, glaring at her sister.

"Only if you're not," Amelia shot back.

"Hurry, girls," Rex called. "Your paintbrushes— and two specially striped candy canes—await! Okay, fine, every kid gets one! But you can't chomp on them till after lunch."

Both Calettis grinned and ran over, their argument canceled for the time being, anyway.

She definitely owed him one.

Chloe still shrieked her head off, which probably helped the twins want to escape being anywhere near Maisey. She kept one eye on Danny, who was intently coloring, elbow holding down the page, left hand over left ear, little tongue out in concentration, as he colored a dog purple and green. She rocked Chloe this way and that, shushing, there-there-ing.

She glanced at Rex, who was in a huddle with his crew. Then he came over to Maisey and held his arms out.

"Bet Chloe needs a change of hands," Rex said. "My sister-in-law Sara taught me that when I'd be over and the twins would be bawling their eyes out. Usually someone new holding them would quiet them right down, a new face to stare at."

Was he actually asking to take her screaming baby? The man was a saint.

She handed over Chloe, who continued to screech. Rex made a funny face at her, which got him a bigger shriek, but then he held her high up in the air, her legs dangling, swooshing her up and down, up and down, and the crying stopped. Maisey almost fell to her knees in relief. Not only did she have the usual full house, but rehearsals for the holiday show would be starting in a half hour, and four kids needed line refreshers between now and then so they wouldn't get upset during the practice run and torpedo the rehearsal—which had happened twice and wasn't pretty.

"I've got this," Rex said to her, giving Chloe a little bounce against his chest. "I've prepped the crew—Annalise and Tyler will pencil in the design while the Calettis paint the big sections. Then they'll all paint in the scene. So I can hold Chloe and supervise. Take care of whatever you need to."

"I owe you," she said. "Home-cooked dinner after the shopping trip tonight?" Alone with Rex in her cabin? After what had happened last night? Maybe making him dinner wasn't a good idea. She could barely resist him and she had to.

But she really, really, really wanted to be alone with him.

"The last time I was in your cabin, I kissed you. And not some giggling-teen-dangling-mistletoe-above-our-heads kiss."

"I know," she said. "I liked it."

"I did, too. But it's like we're gasoline and the kiss is a match. Kaboom."

Heed the warning, Maisey.

"Yeah, yeah, you're leaving town, life on the road. I know. But you have to eat, right? Oh, wait. No match, no worries. Daisy mentioned she's making a big family dinner tonight, remember?"

"Ah, that's right. Another night, then," he said, holding her gaze.

Except there weren't many left.

Ping. Maisey checked her phone. It was a text from Daisy Dawson.

I'm hosting a dinner party at my house tonight in honor of having all my brothers home at the same time. Love you to join. Don't bring anything, just yourself and Chloe. She can hang with the other littles.

Daisy, your timing is, as usual, impeccable. "Turns out I'm invited to dinner," she said, unable to hide her smile.

But Rex wasn't smiling. At all. In fact, he seemed upset. "I told Daisy not to matchmake when she knows I'm leaving. What is she doing?"

Maisey gnawed her lower lip. *Jeez.* Could he want her there less?

"Crud. I probably shouldn't have said that out loud. I didn't mean—"

"Nothing wrong with truth," she interrupted, though she felt foolish for flirting about the kiss and a home-cooked meal. He *was* leaving, dammit. He was right. She needed to get her head out of the clouds when it came to Rex Dawson.

"Daisy probably just invited me as an experienced set of hands and eyes for all the kiddos," she said. "That's one toddler and three babies. This way, you and your family can focus on the reunion and I can pop up and handle any crying and diaper needs."

He didn't seem to be falling for that. Even she knew Daisy hadn't meant the invitation that way.

"You're not the babysitter at the dinner," he said. "You're part of the clan. I see you that way."

She tilted her head. "What way?"

He stared at her for a second, his complexion paling a bit. "Family," he finally said in almost a whisper.

"You see me as family?" Did he? Goose bumps ran up and down her spine. Being part of a family was all she'd ever wanted.

Chloe let out a gurgle, and he rocked her back and forth. "The letter to Santa," he said, "finding you here, you alone in the world except for a six-month-old, needing so much—"

"So you feel bad for me?" she snapped. "Rex, I can take care of myself. I *am* taking care of myself. And my daughter." She reached for Chloe, but the baby's face crumpled and turned red, and Maisey sighed and held up her hands. "She likes where she is right now and I have to work with the kids on their songs, so I guess I'll see you at six for the gift shopping."

"Maisey," he said, but nothing else came out of his mouth.

I am an idiot, she thought. For one shining moment, she'd thought he'd really meant it, that he felt so close to her that she'd become part of him. Like family. But he was only saying that he felt a sense of obligation to her because she was "poor never-adopted broke-and-alone Maisey," whose old Christmas wish letter he'd found.

He saved dogs. He was trying to save her, including her Christmas.

Well, she would save herself, thank you.

She lifted her chin and was about to turn away to escape Rex and find Zara, her song apprentice, when seven-year-old Lara intercepted Maisey, her head down.

"Maisey, my stomach hurts and I don't want to play anymore."

Maisey gave the little girl a once-over. She didn't look ill, she wasn't clutching her tummy and she was standing just fine. Hmm. Lara was possibly overwhelmed by all the noise and activity. "Want to lie down in the nap cave for a little bit and see if you feel better?"

Lara smiled. "I love the nap cave."

All the kids did. It was a twin futon mattress on a padded section with its own orange canopy for privacy. The girl raced off, clearly feeling instantly better, and went inside.

She glanced at Rex. "Well, I do have to help a few kiddos with some forgotten lines. You're sure you don't mind holding on to Chloe and keeping an eye on Lara in the nap cave?"

He seemed grateful she wasn't keeping their interrupted conversation going. But she was done with that. For now, anyway. "I'm a pro uncle of babies and have gotten really good with little kids, too," he reminded her. "Look," he added, gesturing his chin at Chloe, who was perfectly content right now, her eyes curious and alert as she surveyed her world from Rex Dawson's arms.

And you'd make a pro daddy, she thought wistfully.

He's not your future. He's your immediate present—in all senses of the word. But you know what you know about him and his plans. And all this attention on you comes from a place of generosity and his need to serve and protect. It's not about love.

She finally understood. Her question had been answered after all. By him.

Chapter Ten

After rehearsal, which went very well except for two missed lines and one small crying jag from a three-year-old, Maisey finally relaxed. Luckily, the tiny stuffed elves that she and Rex had added to the bounty at Christmasland for props had done wonders for little Tommy and Danny, who liked having something to hold. Chloe had stayed silent except for a few happy gurgles. Rex had gotten her teething toy from Maisey's tote, and Chloe had grabbed on to it. The man truly was a baby whisperer.

He was still here, too, using power tools to build the stage with his apprentices' help. Both

Tyler and Annalise wore hard hats and work gloves and seemed thrilled. The stage was now built and ready for the various pieces of the set to be added. Throughout the morning, she'd caught Rex glancing at her more than a few times. Why did she have to feel so connected to him? Luckily, right now, he pulled together a basketball game for whoever wanted to play, and several of the kids did. Zara was practicing "Frosty the Snowman" lyrics with Danny, who was shaking his little elf and singing "Frotty Noman," which made Zara giggle.

The rough morning, made a bit rougher by having Rex in full view, had been much improved, though, because Zara Harwood had agreed to be in the show and had rehearsed with the group. She'd started out silent and sullen when Maisey had first met her just days ago, and now she was front and center, helping others and being a part of things. Of all Maisey had accomplished with the show, that was a highlight. Maybe *the* highlight.

The door opened and in walked Emily Harwood with a bright smile. Her red curly hair spilled from a yellow wool hat. Emily's gaze landed on Zara, now practicing a different song, her solo, with her prop, a big stuffed candy cane.

"Hi, Zara. Ready for the hike up Clover Mountain?" Emily called over. "According to the tour leader, it's a scavenger hunt, too. Sounds like a lot of fun."

Zara frowned, barely giving Emily a glance. "I just want to stay here for the day. I'm working on my songs."

Emily's smile faltered but she plastered it right back on, and Maisey could tell the woman had been doing a lot of that. The stress was etched on her face. "Honey, it's just an hour hike before lunch. Then I can drop you back here to practice. I'd love to spend some time with you, just us two."

"I want to stay here!" Zara shouted and ran into the nap cave, pulling the little curtains shut.

Emily's shoulders sank.

Maisey hurried over to her. "Zara opened up to me a little because I shared with her that I lost my parents when I was very young. I grew up in a few different group foster homes. If I can help in any way, I want to."

Emily looked relieved. "We officially adopted Zara almost a year ago, a couple months after she lost her parents. We finally reached a great place where Zara was asking me a lot of questions about calling me Mom and if she should or if that would make her mother in heaven feel bad." Emily's eyes welled with tears. "Things were good for us as a family. But these last few weeks have been rough and nothing I say or try works."

"Could it be the time of year?" Maisey asked. "My parents died in December and some letters to Santa went unanswered, so it's always been a rough time for me, and I'm twenty-three."

"I've tried a lot of holiday approaches, but she's so resistant. I just want her to be comfortable— and happy."

"Would you like me to try to help her open up a little? Small steps. But just agreeing to be in the show is huge, I now realize."

Emily nodded, her expression so full of hope. "Should I let her stay here instead of insisting on the scavenger hike? Sometimes I'm so unsure how to proceed."

"I know what you mean. I think she'll just close up on the hike. Her head is in the show right now, so why don't we keep that happy vibe going and I'll talk to her."

"Thanks, Maisey. I appreciate your help."

She'd broken through some—maybe between her experience and understanding Zara and a slow approach, she could do some good. She headed over to the nap cave and knelt down to let Zara know her mom said it was okay to stay here and that she'd pick her up for lunch in an hour and a half.

Zara scooted out of the cave on her knees and looked around. "Really? She's letting me stay? She already left?" She sat down in front of the tent.

Maisey nodded and sat beside her. "She'll be back to pick you up for lunch," she repeated since Zara seemed surprised Emily had gone. Ah, Zara was very attached to Emily, she realized; that was clear. And good.

"I know your mom is going to miss you on the hike, but I'm happy you're staying. I could sure use your help with Danny on 'Frosty.' Think you can teach him to say 'Snowman' instead of 'Noman'?"

Zara burst out laughing. "I'll try. He's soooo cute."

"Yup, he is."

"Maisey? Can you call Emily Emily and not my mom?"

Maisey nodded. "Of course."

"I mean, she's technically my mom now because she and Ethan adopted me, but it's not like I don't have a mom and dad—they're just not here anymore." Her expression got very serious, but her eyes were clear.

"I used to think about that for myself," Maisey said. "When I was eight, I wrote a letter to Santa asking for a family to adopt me since I'd been at the group foster home since I was five. I wondered if I'd be able to call my new parents Mom and Dad."

Zara peered up at her. "I thought you said you grew up in different group homes, though."

"Yup, I did. I never was adopted, so I don't know how I would have felt about calling someone else Mom."

"I'm sorry you didn't get adopted," Zara said. "I wouldn't want to live in a foster home."

Maisey gave Zara's hand a squeeze. "The hardest time was Christmas. It's a tough time for you, too, huh?"

Zara looked down and nodded, and Maisey could feel the girl stiffen beside her.

Maisey nodded, too. "I used to avoid the whole season. But now that I have Chloe, having Christmas for her is important. New traditions."

Zara looked at her. "What's a tradition?"

"Well, like having a tree and decorating it is a Christmas tradition. Carving a pumpkin is a Halloween tradition. I used to French braid my hair every Monday when I was a teenager because I wanted to make a tradition of my own. I did that for years."

"Do I have traditions?" Zara asked.

"I'm sure you do. What's something that Emily and Ethan do over and over? Like chocolate chip pancakes for breakfast every Saturday morning."

"Well, Ethan gets bagels and cream cheese every Saturday morning. I go with him and get to pick the kinds. My favorite is cinnamon raisin. But not with cream cheese. Just butter. And every Saturday night after dinner, the three of us and our dog, Poppy, watch a movie together and I get to pick that, too."

"There you go! Two family traditions on the same day every week!"

Zara smiled. "Yeah. I didn't really ever think of it like that. But I guess I have traditions."

"Maywee," Danny called from where he was flying his superhero lion around on a big section of the mat. "Frotty Noman jolly pol."

Zara grinned. "Oh, he needs me."

"Yes, he does," Maisey said, her heart pinging like crazy.

Zara bounced up and went over to him.

"Okay, I'm not crying. You're crying," Rex whispered as he walked over.

Maisey had been aware that Rex was still in the Kid Zone, but he seemed so intent on the work he was doing on the stage. "You heard all that?"

"Well, I was supposedly immersed in my work with this hot-glue gun and plywood, but yes. Every word. You handled that really beautifully. Tough stuff, and you were amazing."

Maisey let out a breath. "It's so important to get it right, so thank you. I feel like I say that a lot to you."

"That mean you're not mad at me anymore?" he asked.

"Just don't ever feel sorry for me, Rex Dawson. I won't allow it."

Did he have to look at her that way? As though she was very special to him?

"Got it," he said. "And I don't. I just—"

She waited, but he didn't finish.

I just care about you. She knew that was what he'd been about to say.

Ditto, she thought, her heart pinging again.

Since dinner at Daisy's was at seven thirty, Rex and Maisey decided to go to Bear Ridge for gift shopping; there was a cute shop open late for the season that carried a lot of baby and kids' toys and interesting little items. When they dropped off Chloe at Daisy's house, his sister cooed baby talk, telling Chloe in a running commentary that she'd be watching her until her mama returned and how much fun dinner would be later, that she'd hang at the baby table with her new besties.

"I don't know what I did to deserve you Dawsons, but thank you," Maisey said, beaming at Daisy.

You deserve everything. You deserve all the happiness in the world. And I can give it to you up to a point, he thought with a frown as they got back in his SUV and headed to town. Luckily, Maisey was chatty on the ride, going over the list they'd made, and he was distracted from his thoughts, which seemed all blurry lately. Yes, his job was important to him, and he used to love being on the road, no real home base. But now everything felt *different* in a way he wasn't... ready to accept.

His feelings for Maisey, for one.

And some other complicated stuff he didn't want to think about. Rex thought he liked change since his entire life was about change. But in reality, he didn't.

At the gift shop, she and Rex split the list, Rex taking the boys and Maisey the girls. There was a basketball alarm clock that played hip-hop music—Tyler, check. A new superhero coloring book and big pack of crayons for Danny—done. Rex was surprisingly good at shopping for various ages, though he had no idea where he'd picked up the skill. Maisey met him at the cashier's counter with a pair of fuzzy purple slippers for Annalise, the music note pin for Zara, and a double check of their list showed they'd gotten all ten regulars gifts.

"I checked their ornaments on the display, but no Siamese cat," she said. "But at least I have this cute thing for Chloe," she added, holding up the cat-shaped teething toy she'd gotten her.

The shop offered to wrap, but that would take forever, so Maisey said she'd do the wrapping herself tonight, adding a few rolls and tape to the counter. Then they headed out and loaded up the car.

"We have a solid half hour left," she said. "You know what I'd like to do? See where you found my bottle with my letter to Santa. If it's close enough."

He nodded. "It's about ten minutes from here. Bear Ridge Nature Preserve."

"I'd just like to see where it ended up. Not that we can know how long it was there. Maybe it got stuck a bunch of times and then moved and then stayed put by the footbridge. But it definitely didn't get far in fifteen years."

Rex rounded the car when he heard someone call his name. He turned around and groaned inwardly. Patrick Mullers. His dad's old drinking and gambling buddy.

"Hey, Rex, right? How ya doin'?" Patrick asked, coming over with a big smile. The few times he'd run into Patrick over the years, the man had called him by one brother's name or another. But this time he'd gotten it right. Patrick looked a lot better these days. Face wasn't so red, belly wasn't so extended. Maybe he'd stopped drinking.

"This is Maisey Clark. Maisey, Patrick Mullers. He was my dad's good friend."

Maisey smiled and shook his hand.

"I miss that crazy lunatic," Patrick said. "Do you know I got cleaned up after we lost him? A few of us did, his old drinking pals. Scared us half to death and we didn't want to get to the other half faster."

"I'm glad to hear it," Rex said. He really was.

"I'll never forget the time your dad and I took you seahorse searching in the river by the cabins at the ranch. Remember that? You were obsessed. Bo insisted there was a family of seahorses that lived in this one spot in the river, a father with six kids—five sons and a daughter."

A vague memory floated into Rex's mind. He had been very into seahorses when he was a little kid, around seven or eight. He forgot all about that. "Hey, wait—yes, he said the seahorses were the Fishly family. I think he even named them all."

"Yup, that's right. The Fishly seahorses. I remember we took you there to look for them and your dad insisted he saw the dad seahorse swimming around but that Pa Seahorse got scared and hid. You were so happy they were real that you said he was the best dad ever. Later Bo told me that was the only time any of his kids ever said that."

Rex could barely find his voice for a second. "I remember that. I didn't know I was the only one to say it. Ever." He glanced at Maisey, glad she was here. Because he felt like absolute hell.

"Well, you were only seven or so, so I'm sure someone else said it in the following years. He loved you kids." He glanced behind him at his truck. Someone was in the passenger seat. "The lady is waiting, so I'd better go. Good to see you, Rex. Nice to meet you, Maisey."

Rex watched him walk away, his stomach churning. "Seahorses. The Fishly family. Hearing you're the best dad ever for the first time. Maybe the only time."

Maisey squeezed his hand. "Well, I'm just glad he heard it. That his child said it to him. And yes, another kid probably did at some point after. Sounds like Bo Dawson was capable of great things as a dad, Rex."

He nodded. "Yeah, I suppose he had his moments. Don't know how I could forget something like that."

"I do. Repression. Memories get socked away when they're too big to deal with, even the good memories. Especially when your memories of someone are complicated."

He reached for her and she opened her arms for a hug. A quick hug over too soon. "I'm glad you're here."

She gave him a gentle smile. "Me, too."

"Let's get over to the nature preserve," he said. "I'll show you where I found the bottle—and my dog."

My dog. My dog. My dog.

He was going to walk away from River? How? And his family? And Maisey?

Maybe having a reason to come back to visit more often was a good thing. The pull to home. Like Maisey said: *complicated.*

He drove to the nature preserve and parked pretty much where he had last month. Once again, not a soul was here, though he'd parked to avoid public view the first time around. "There's a trail that's not tended well but it's there enough to follow. It leads to the footbridge."

They walked over, and every time the cold wind lifted her hair he wanted to wrap her scarf tighter, keep her warm, protect her from any tiny or big harm. After five minutes they arrived at the short bridge over the river. She followed him to the spot where he'd first seen River, sniffing and pawing at the bottle.

"Right there," he said, pointing.

Almost six weeks ago, his entire life had changed when he'd noticed the cute shepherd mix, dirty and hungry and lonely, scratching at the bottle. Of course he was fighting against that change—his life was outside of the Dawson Family Guest Ranch, outside of Maisey Clark and her baby.

She looked down over the wood railing of the bridge to where he indicated. "I can remember writing that letter, tossing the bottle in the creek with my friend, like it was yesterday. Well, maybe not yesterday. More like a few years ago. It feels so recent, so much like a part of me still. How can that be?"

"Probably because of how much you wanted what you asked for." He'd felt that yearning brimming from the paper when he'd held it in his hands, felt it in his cells.

She looked at him and nodded. "I do feel like that eight-year-old girl sometimes. More than sometimes. Even lately."

This was about him, he guessed. And his family. What they were coming to mean to her? What *he* meant to her?

"And you turned out to be my Santa," she said. "In its own way, I feel like that letter got answered. Not with parents. But with...a tribe of my own.

That's how I feel at the Dawson Family Guest Ranch, Rex. Like the place and all of you are my people. Like I belong."

His thoughts had been on the right track. "I wasn't kidding when I said you were family, Maisey. You've become part of the place." *A part of me.*

Tears filled her eyes and he opened his arms. He hugged her for a solid minute, resting his chin on her head, breathing in the scent of her shampoo and the cold snap of air around them.

"Thanks for showing me," she said with a sniffle. "And just thank you."

He gave her an extra squeeze, wishing he could hold her forever. But they had to get back. Family dinner. And she was indeed going.

Yeah, he knew he was leaving on the twenty-sixth. But it was going to be a lot harder than he'd ever thought.

Chapter Eleven

"Would you mind dropping me off at my cabin?" Maisey asked as they pulled up to the gates of the ranch. "I have just enough time for a quick shower and to change out of my work clothes. I think I have an orange handprint on my calf and glitter on my sleeve."

He held out his arm and rolled up his own sleeve. "Purple glitter in this one spot. I scrubbed but it won't come off. I kinda like it. And sure, I'll watch Chloe for you. Then we'll walk over to Daisy's."

Of course he'd watch Chloe and sit around waiting for Maisey—because he was That Guy. The ole prince among men. She'd barely had a boyfriend in high school, and her husband had been her "first" in just about every sense. When she'd stand up for herself, he'd constantly respond that "this is how guys are, Maze." She knew that couldn't be the case. Her dad had also been a prince, so she'd *known*. But she'd chosen wrong out of such a deep yearning to belong, and now she had to choose right to keep her heart from getting so broken that she might not be able to pick herself up again.

No, of course she would get right up again. She'd have to. She was someone's mother and that role came first. As amazing a man as Rex was, his point in her life seemed to be to remind her that her dad wasn't the only one of his kind. There were good, great men out there.

Not that that made her feel better *now*.

She hurried into her bathroom, taking the quickest shower possible, a trick she'd learned as a new mother. She blow-dried her hair and put on a little makeup, then rushed across the hall to her bedroom and put on a long off-white sweater with a beaded V-neckline, skinny black jeans—which she'd just started fitting into again—and boots. Plus a dab of perfume behind her ears.

Rex stood up when she came back into the living room, and she was well aware that he was staring at her. "You look great. And smell great."

She smiled. "Not like paint and glue and baby spit-up and pretzel dust?"

"Like flowers."

She liked that he noticed.

They bundled back up in coats, scarves, hats and gloves, and Maisey grabbed the loaf of Portuguese bread that they'd stopped for at the bakery in town, then headed into the December night air. He held out his arm. She wrapped hers around it and looked up at the stars. If only this was as it looked, she thought, imagining that anyone who saw them together right now would assume they were a couple.

Up ahead she could just make out the Harwood family heading from the cabins on the path to the cafeteria. Zara was actually walking between them instead of lagging behind, head down, as she usually was when Maisey spotted her out with the parents. A good sign.

"I think things are going to be okay there," she said, upping her chin at the family as they went into the cafeteria.

"You did a lot of good. You got involved. You opened up. You bridged a connection. Zara might not have realized that she could be living in foster care if not for the Harwoods. You said it without saying it outright."

She glanced at him, the illumination from the

tall iron streetlamps casting beautiful shadows on his face. He was always her champion. Something she'd never had before. She hadn't even known she'd been missing such a force in her life. Someone she thought was special, someone she respected, respected her right back.

"One thing I've come to understand is that everything's relative to someone else's situation," she said, thinking of a couple of her former foster sisters. "Just because I wanted to be adopted and wasn't doesn't mean Zara should be grateful she was adopted when she's struggling with having new parents. I knew two kids who were adopted and it wasn't all sunshine and roses, so that helped me understand Zara better. Eight-year-old me would have thought she was a brat for not being grateful. But now I get it."

"She's lucky you do. And I'm sure the Harwoods appreciate that she has you to talk to."

Maisey stopped walking as she was thunderstruck by the notion that she loved this man. She knew she'd fallen in love with him, but now that love enveloped her. How was she going to say goodbye in just a few days?

As they neared the farmhouse, Rex sniffed the air. "Hmm, I can smell something delicious cooking from here. Which means Harrison is in the kitchen tonight. I love Daisy, but she usually burns everything."

Maisey laughed. "I'm starving. And I can't wait to see Chloe. It feels so strange to be walking around without her, someone else taking care of her. I feel both carefree and completely anxious."

"I guess that's motherhood for you. I don't even want to think about how overprotective I'd be as a dad. 'Chloe, you're not dating till you're twenty-five and that's final!'" He laughed, then seemed to realize what he'd said and cleared his throat. "Not that I'll *be* Chloe's dad. I mean... Well, you know what I mean. Just an example." He nodded and quickened his pace.

A few days ago all that might have nicked her feelings, reminding her that he *wouldn't* ever be Chloe's dad. But now she found herself smiling to herself because the man was tripping over himself. And something else was coming clear: he didn't know what he wanted anymore.

These thoughts would have to wait till she was alone in bed tonight because they were suddenly up the porch steps, greeted by River and Dude and welcomed inside by Daisy.

Inside were many Dawsons. Ranch manager Noah and his forewoman wife, Sara, and their twin babies, Annabel and Chance. Guest relations manager Daisy and her businessman husband,

Harrison, and their baby, Tony. Safety director and wilderness tour guide Axel and his wife, ranch nutritionist Sadie, and their toddler, Danny. Plus Zeke, also a businessman, and Ford, a cop. Maisey was about to add Rex and herself and Chloe to the count when she realized she was invited because she was an employee who cared for their children and she'd gotten somewhat close with Daisy.

She wasn't "with" Rex here. *And don't you forget it, no matter how much he seems up in the air with what he wants from life.*

Daisy gave her a big hug, gave the loaf of bread to Harrison to slice for the table and brought her into the living room, where Chloe and Tony were in Exersaucers, and Annabel and Chance were sitting close by on a mat, playing with big foam blocks. Eight-month-old Annabel and Chance were two months older than Chloe, who was a month older than Tony. Two-year-old Danny sat with his legs out in front of him, teaching them the words to "Frotty Noman," which had the room in a fit of giggles.

"Baby Central!" Zeke said, scooping up Annabel while Ford picked up Chance. They both snuggled their niece and nephew, then did the same with Tony and Danny. Like all the Dawson brothers, Zeke had dark hair and blue eyes.

"And who's this beautiful little girl?" Ford asked.

"She's mine," Maisey said. "I'm the new head nanny at the Kid Zone. I guess Chloe and I are crashing the family dinner."

"You're such a big part of our kiddos' lives that you felt like family fast," Daisy said, sitting down beside the mat and petting River and ruffling Dude's soft fur. The dogs both sat beside her on the floor, guarding the babies. "That makes you an honorary Dawson."

Maisey smiled but she had to home in on the *felt like* and *honorary*. She wasn't *really* part of this family. She was an employee, and the Dawsons were good and generous people, so she was here.

Suddenly that old yearning was back. To be part of a family. This one.

After dinner, which was a hearty beef stew that Rex had had two helpings of, the group moved into the living room for coffee and dessert, scattering around the big room. During dinner, Maisey had jumped up every time a child fussed, but one of his brothers always beat her to it. Rex loved watching it sink in for her that she'd truly been invited as a guest—not a babysitter.

Now she sat with Sara and Sadie in the group of chairs in the far corner of the room, and he couldn't hear what they were talking about. Hopefully not him. Daisy was on the love seat with Noah, Axel and Zeke. Rex looked around for Ford and found him in the kitchen, loading up the dishwasher.

"Hiding out?" Rex asked with a grin.

"From Daisy. Every time she comes near me I zigzag away so she can't ask me about my love life or the openings at the Bear Ridge PD."

Rex handed him two dirty plates from the counter. "Are you going to join the force here?"

Ford stood still for a second. "I'm ninety percent yes on that. I need to get out of Casper. Something new. Fresh start."

Huh. Ford had always been the most vocal about wanting to get as far from this place as possible, but even his eldest brother had had to admit that nothing about the renovated ranch, now a truly gorgeous piece of property, reminded him of sadder days gone by.

"Law enforcement will be a lot different in a town this small," Rex said.

"That would be a welcome change, too. But the ole serve and protect can be done anywhere there are people. You thinking about coming home, too?"

"Me? Nah. I mean, I've thought about it because the subject has come up. That goes without saying when you're around Daisy." He smiled but felt it fade fast. "Since I was a teenager I wanted to be a cop. Like you." He'd always looked up to

Ford, who was almost five years older. "And then that crazy gambling buddy of Dad's went on that robbery spree and eluded capture. I kept thinking he'd come seek revenge on us in our sleep because Dad swindled him in a poker game. Remember that?"

"Oh, I remember," Ford said, adding a bunch of silverware to the basket in the dishwasher. "Dad was worried sick. The marshals got him a day later." He glanced at Rex. "Is that why you wanted to become a marshal? Track down fugitives? Because of that?"

Rex nodded. "I felt so powerless back then. I couldn't do anything, keep anyone I cared about safe. Now it's my job to do so."

"Yeah, I feel that way, too. But I can do that from here. *Closer* to the people I care about."

There it was again, that *feeling* Rex couldn't quite name. Unsettled. Uncomfortable. Itchy. If he liked the Dawson Family Guest Ranch, liked Bear Ridge, liked being here, and he did, what the hell was the problem? Why was he burning to leave?— and he *was*. That force in him wasn't just about his job; he knew that. So what was this really about?

His father? How rough a lot of his childhood was during his visitation weekends here at the ranch? Maybe all the renovations in the world couldn't fix what lurked underneath: really bad memories. But then a good one would come along, prompted by someone else, like his father's friend had done today, and Rex would be just as uneasy on the subject of his father. He'd loved his father and had hated him. How did you reconcile that? Especially when the person in question was gone.

He could talk to Ford about this. He could talk to any of his siblings, and even the more reticent when it came to deeply personal stuff would let loose about Bo Dawson. But sometimes there was like a cork stuffed somewhere in Rex where he couldn't get anything out.

"Speaking of Dad," Rex said, handing him two bowls. "I still can't figure out what the key he left me opens."

If he could just find the thing already, maybe it would help. Maybe he'd get some closure.

Ford nodded. "I've been trying to follow the map he left me, which indicates where he supposedly buried my mother's old diary that pissed him off for some reason he didn't mention, but I can't find it. Either the map is wrong or I'm just not thinking about it the way Dad would. He wasn't exactly map-oriented or linear. The X and the landmarks he scribbled are probably completely off. He was likely drunk when he drew the map."

No doubt. "I'll help you look if you want," Rex said.

"The ground's too hard to poke or dig in now. Just as well. Who knows what the hell I'll read in that diary—if I find it."

Rex nodded, and for a moment, they just both stood there trying to wrap their minds around it all. "I ran into one of Dad's old poker pals earlier tonight in town. Patrick Mullers. He reminded me of a story about how he and Dad took me seahorse spotting at the river where he said he'd seen a family of them. Across from that big boulder our guests like to sit on to stargaze and make out. Patrick told me I said Dad was the best dad ever while we were there and that Bo was really moved."

"I'm sure he was. Not like Bo Dawson heard that every day. Or ever. Because he wasn't."

Rex nodded again and handed Ford two more plates—and was suddenly struck by a memory. His dad had surprised him with a small fish tank with two seahorses, bright blue gravel, some plants and a treasure chest cave for his eighth birthday, not long after the day at the river. Rex had loved the way the seahorses swam upright and turned into the colors of the plants, green and coral. The seahorses hadn't lived long, though, and Rex had moved on to being obsessed with playing hockey and baseball. He'd all but forgotten about that tank, but he was surprised he had. Maisey was likely right about that little coping mechanism called repression. Made it easier not to be grief-stricken.

He thought about his mom dropping him off at his dad's the evening of his birthday, Diana gently reminding him that his dad was forgetful and if he didn't remember to get Rex a gift that it didn't mean his father didn't love him. Rex had walked in the farmhouse expecting nothing, maybe not even a "happy birthday." But right there on a table in the living room was the tank with a big blue bow on top and a hand-scrawled sign that read Property of Rex Dawson, Age 8.

"Whoa," Rex said, going completely still.

Ford turned to him. "What?"

"There's a small tank in the attic. It must have been the one he bought me for my eighth birthday. It was under an old table and there was stuff in the tank—I don't remember what, a bunch of junk. Maybe the key opens something in it?" Rex shrugged, but suddenly the idea didn't seem nuts or even far-fetched. It seemed like something Bo Dawson would do.

Ford's eyes widened. "Later, dishwasher. Let's go see."

Rex followed him into the living room. "Let me just go tell Maisey I'll be back in a bit."

Ford raised an eyebrow. "Oh, I didn't realize you two were together."

Are we? he wondered. "Well, we came together. So…"

Ford grinned. "Go tell your lady."

She is my lady. For now, Rex thought. He found Maisey standing by the Christmas tree, Chloe in her arms, pointing out the colors of the lights.

"Hey," he said. "Mind if I disappear on you for a few minutes? I want to go check something out in the attic with Ford."

"Sure, go ahead. I'm fine. See you in a few."

He nodded and gave Chloe's back a quick caress, all too aware that he didn't have to check in with Maisey. But he had. Everything meant something these days.

He met Ford at the door to the attic and they headed upstairs.

"Under that?" Ford asked, pointing to the rickety old rectangular table that looked like it could barely hold the boxes of assorted junk on it.

Rex knelt down in front of the table and shoved aside another box, and there it was—the fish tank with more junk inside it. Rex slid out the tank and took the other boxes off the table and put the tank on top to make it easier to go through.

He reached in and removed a half-smashed Sony Walkman that had to be from the '80s. A bunch of batteries, a few rusted metal tape measures, a half bag of blue gravel that must have been from the original tank and a ratty kitchen towel. With something wrapped in it.

Rex glanced at Ford and threw off the towel. Bingo. A small tackle box with a lock.

"How'd he expect you to go digging in here?" Ford asked, shaking his head. "If you hadn't run into his poker buddy, you never would've remembered the seahorses in the first place."

Maybe not. But maybe he would have. He'd been sharing so much with Maisey about his dad that memory after memory had been unearthed. He would have hit on the seahorses and remembered he'd seen the tank up here and that maybe his father put something lockable inside it. He was just relieved he'd found it.

Then again, the key had to work in it.

He fished the key out of his wallet. "Here goes everything," he said and pushed it into the lock. "I don't believe it."

"Classic Dad," Ford said, half smiling, half shaking his head. "If Daisy ever held a yard sale for stuff in here, that's when she would have found the box, not been able to open it and probably tossed it aside until someone tried to jimmy it open. Why would he have been so lax about you finding it?"

"He probably figured I'd spend some time trying to figure out what the key unlocked and go through my old stories until I hit on possibilities. He ended up right. Hey, it only took an entire year."

Ford grinned. "Open it. I'm dying to know."

"Me, too." Rex turned the key and inside the tackle box was what appeared to be a children's pocket watch. It was yellow, made out of plastic and was on a long matching chain. Rex opened it. There was a cartoon illustration of a smiling seahorse and underneath read *It's time for fun!* Around the dial were clock numbers, one through twelve. Rex stared at it and held it up for Ford. Also in the box was a folded-up piece of lined paper.

Rex took in a breath and unfolded it.

Rex,
If you found this, then you remembered your
old seahorse tank. I'll never forget the day
I took you to see the seahorse family in the
river—I can't remember what I named them,
something funny. That day you said I was
the best dad ever even though you didn't see
any seahorses. You believed me that they

were there and I can't even remember the
last time anyone believed something I said.
That day stayed with me a long time. Till
the end, clearly.

Anyway, couple months ago I saw this
kiddie pocket watch at a yard sale a girl-
friend was having and I bought it for fifty
cents. I don't know where you are or what
you're doing but I know you've been on the
road a long time, chasing old ghosts, most
likely. I'm probably right about that even
though I get mostly everything wrong these
days. Anyway, you'll find this eventually,
one day, and when you do, just know your
father loved you, Rexy.
Dad

Tears stung the backs of Rex's eyes and he
quickly handed the note to Ford, then moved a
few feet over to the tiny round window that over-
looked the side yard to get ahold of himself.

A half minute later, he felt Ford clap an arm
around his shoulders. "When Bo Dawson got it
right, he really knocked it out of the park, didn't
he." He tucked the folded page into Rex's shirt
pocket.

Rex could only nod.

"I'll give you some time," Ford said. "Come on down when you're ready."

He heard his brother's footsteps on the stairs and the door at the bottom close. Rex sucked in another breath.

Was he chasing old ghosts? That was what had gotten him started in the US Marshals, maybe, but his commitment to his job had long been about justice for all. He could feel the letter in his pocket and suddenly it felt heavy. He took it out and put it in his wallet, next to the key.

His father was the old ghost here, haunting him right now. Up and down, good and bad, right and wrong. Bad love and good. *Just know your father loved you, Rexy.*

The attic was making him claustrophobic, so he took the pocket watch out of the box and dropped that in his shirt pocket, then closed the box and put it back in the tank. He left the tank on the table; there was no rhyme or reason to the boxes being here or there, anyway.

He'd come up here looking for what the key unlocked to find some peace about his dad and instead just felt all kinds of conflicted.

Suddenly he just wanted to go home. And that was when it hit him. He had no home.

Chapter Twelve

Maisey had gotten home hours ago from Daisy's dinner party and she still couldn't get the image out of her mind of Rex carrying Chloe the short walk from the farmhouse to the cabin, her baby girl snuggled against his leather jacket. She'd tried to distract herself with tidying up the kitchen, starting a new mystery novel she'd taken out of the library and then flipping channels, but she kept seeing that image. Rex Dawson holding her baby girl so tenderly, so carefully.

And then practically running out the door of her cabin once Chloe was back in Maisey's arms and they were inside.

Something had happened in the attic that Rex didn't want to talk about, and she had the feeling it had something to do with his father. She knew he'd been looking for whatever the key his dad had left him opened. Maybe he'd found it. She had no idea, though, because he hadn't said more than ten words on the way home. That was unusual for him, so she'd given him his space.

Now, in her jammies in bed, she turned on the lamp on her bedside table and grabbed her phone. She couldn't take it anymore; she had to have some communication with him, even a text that he might not respond to till morning. He *would* respond because he was Rex Dawson.

Thanks again for all your help today and shopping tonight. The kids are going to love their gifts. Had a great time at dinner with your family.

She turned off the lamp, put her phone on her chest and hoped for a ping.

Ping.

She smiled and lifted the phone.

Always my pleasure, M. I'll be at the Kid Zone at nine for the dress rehearsal to make sure everything with the set is okay and I can help out as needed.

She waited, hoping those three little dots would appear to indicate he was still typing. She wanted something personal. Something that wasn't about the show or the sets. Something about *them*.

Well, you weren't personal, either, she reminded herself.

She texted: You okay? If you need to talk, I'm here.

A-OK was all he wrote back. Then the three dots appeared, which got her excited. Until she read: See you tomorrow.

Shut out. Or that was how it felt. She pulled the comforter up to her chin and closed her eyes, but she knew she wasn't going to get a great night's sleep.

In the morning, Maisey got herself and Chloe up early to get to the Kid Zone so that she could make sure everything was set for the holiday show before the kids piled in—and so she could be there for a bit before Rex came in all gorgeous and helpful and driving her bonkers.

Tomorrow was the Christmas fair, which would start at nine and would end at four. The children's holiday show would start at five. For the past two days, she'd had rehearsals at that time, too, to make sure the littlest kids could handle that hour, and so far, so good. The kids' gifts were wrapped and tagged with their names and waiting in a locked closet across the hall in the lodge. The sets were done, sturdy and adorable. The props were in baskets on either side of the stage, which had one riser, the taller kids on the second row, the shorter ones in front.

Maisey walked around the room with Chloe still in her chest carrier. "We did it," she said. "We pulled it off in pretty short time. Just think, Chloe, not too long from now, you'll be running around the Kid Zone, building towers out of blocks, hanging out in the nap cave, appearing in the holiday show your own mother started."

She smiled and spun around, taking in the gorgeously decorated room, truly merry and bright. The tree on the side of the stage was twinkling with multicolored lights, a gold star atop. A big wreath hung on the wall behind the colorful stage. And the other walls were bordered by garland.

"All right, I'm ready for the kids, rehearsal and Rex Dawson," she whispered, walking Chloe over to her bassinet since the baby was about ready for her morning nap.

She'd just gotten Chloe settled when the door opened and children and parents poured in, waving hellos, signing in at the front desk, various kids wrapping Maisey in hugs. She loved these hugs so much.

No matter what was going on with her relationship with Rex, she was lucky to have this perfect-for-her job and she'd count her blessings on December 26 when he walked out the door for the last time and wouldn't return. For a few months, anyway, until it was time to visit for a relative's birthday or a special event.

The door opened again and there he was, as usual so handsome and sexy in his black leather jacket and the plaid red scarf, his dark hair a gorgeous contrast with his fair skin and blue eyes.

He waved and she waved back. Then he gave the stage and riser a solid once-over and jumped hard on it a few times, testing for sturdiness. The stage passed his test.

He kept his distance all day, through the dress rehearsal and even through her break, when he was nowhere to be found. So much for having a quick cup of coffee together just so she could try to figure out what was going on. Then again, what was going on was clear. He was avoiding her. Something happened last night that had gotten to him, and he was retreating.

From her, if not from his promise to lend a hand when she and her staffers got very busy during the day. He'd come to the rescue for a couple of meltdowns, including one by his nephew Danny. When she was busy helping a group with their songs, he picked up a fussing Chloe and rocked her for fifteen minutes.

He was his usual helpful self.

His usual there's-nothing-going-on-between-us self. He'd never really veered from that; she'd just suffered from wishful thinking.

By the end of the day, he'd checked in a couple of times by text—did they need anything last-minute? He could run to Prairie City, where the big-box store stayed open late.

He, not we. The man was definitely distancing himself from her, but she had the feeling it had nothing to do with her. Sometimes *It's not you, it's me* really did apply. But in this case, Rex was getting in his own way. Holding on to truths he might have outgrown.

Maybe that was just wishful thinking, too. His job was elsewhere; his life was elsewhere. He'd never said any different, never led her to believe otherwise.

He'd agreed to help out with the show and had. Everything was done; everything was set.

Including the two of them. Done. He was leaving.

Rex felt like hell. He was supposed to be giving Maisey Christmas back, and instead he was acting like a real jerk. Avoiding her. Making himself scarce. She didn't deserve that from him.

With his dog sniffing along the riverbank in front of him, Rex sat on the big boulder in front of the water near the guest cabins, hoping none of them would come along and engage him in small talk. He wasn't in the mood, couldn't put on his cheery face and talk about the history of the ranch back when his grandparents first opened it. The guests loved hearing about the fifty-year run of the place before it had been completely renovated.

He just wanted to sit here, just ten feet from where his father had pointed out the Fishly family of seahorses, trying to make his young son happy. Last night, after he'd walked Maisey home, also barely saying two words to her, he'd gone back to the farmhouse, not wanting to be there, but at least he had a small guest room there with a door he could close so he could just…think. Try to figure out what was eating him.

But Zeke had come knocking. His brothers and sister were having a nightcap of spiked eggnog in the living room and "you'd better come or else."

The spiked eggnog had him unwinding just enough to say too much, which was why he rarely drank at all. He'd told Ford that sometimes he thought his problem was that he was tired of the stress and travel of his job and that it made him feel disloyal—to his personal mission to hunt down fugitives, to his team.

Ford had said that people grow and change and evolve, a necessary part of life, and no one had to work the same job for forty years and get a toaster or a watch like in their grandparents' time. If Ford could change his mind about coming home to the ranch, Rex could, he said. *If* that was what Rex wanted, his brother had been quick to add.

Staying would be about Maisey, though. And he wasn't looking for a commitment. He'd never wanted a commitment. When he'd tried it because he'd fallen for someone, all he'd ended up doing was hurting her because he still couldn't see himself, imagine himself, married to someone. His life, for the longest time, had been about *leaving*. Not staying. Not ties that bound.

"Hey, just the man I needed," came a familiar voice.

Rex turned to find Tyler, the thirteen-year-old star dribbler, carrying his ball and walking toward him. He liked Tyler and was so tired of his own head that he welcomed the distraction right now.

River padded over for a pat on the head and along his side, which he got. Rex tossed a biscuit closer to the water, and the pooch beelined for it, stretching out to enjoy his treat.

"Hey, Tyler. What can I do for you?"

"I need advice about the ladies. One lady. Well, a girl."

Rex tried not to grin too hard. Tyler was a really sweet kid, dramatic but earnest and sensitive, though most people probably didn't realize it.

Tyler pushed up the rim of his ski hat a bit. "So here's the thing. I really like Annalise but I don't think she likes me back. First of all, I'm a whole year younger. And she's two inches taller. And she lives in Utah. So how am I gonna make this happen?"

This time Rex couldn't help his smile. "Well, you could tell her how you feel. And see what happens. Maybe she'll surprise you."

"Right. She just happens to like younger, shorter guys?"

"Maybe she just likes *you*, Tyler. There's plenty to like."

"Yeah?" he asked, tilting his head. "Everyone says I'm funny. And nice. But that usually means friend-zone." He stared at the river for a moment. "Tell me how you got Maisey to like you. I mean, you're taller and maybe older, but she's really pretty. Like Annalise."

"Maisey and I aren't a couple. We're just friends. But she likes me because I'm nice, too. And also funny, if I do say so myself. And because we have things in common. Basic chemistry, really." *A chemistry that's more powerful than I am.* "But if you like Annalise, if you want to stay in touch once you both leave, you need to tell her how you feel. Maybe you'll end up just friends. But that's good, too."

Except when it came to him and Maisey, *just friends* felt so wrong, so inadequate for what was between them. Rex had always been a very controlled person—he was aware of that and it was a good trait for his work. If he let loose, really let himself go with Maisey, he'd lose that control, equilibrium. Like now, the way this unfinished, unsettled business with his dad had him feeling. Off-kilter. Wrong.

"So I just say, 'Annalise, I really like you. Can we try a long-distance romance?'"

Rex smiled. "Sure. She may say no, Tyler. But you've got to be in it to win it."

"First rule of basketball," he said, giving the ball a bounce. He popped up off the rock. "Thanks, bro. I owe you."

"Anytime," Rex said and watched the boy head up the path toward his cabin, tossing the ball in the air every few steps.

He turned back to the river. Both of them—the water and his dog. *His dog.* Those words, together in a sentence, *his* applied to him, always caught him off guard, always stopped him in his tracks.

I can't even think of the best dog in the world as mine without having some kind of panic attack, he realized. He wasn't going anywhere near the words *committed relationship*.

Let alone *wife*.

He'd thought coming down here and checking out where the fictitious Fishly family of seahorses had swum would help him figure things out. But he was just as conflicted. His neglectful, alcoholic, complicated dad had loved him, even if part-time. He knew that. He was old enough to understand the beast of addiction and had long stopped taking personally anything Bo Dawson had done. So maybe this wasn't about his father at all *or* believing he wasn't meant to be part of a committed couple since he'd grown up seeing relationships fall apart for one reason or another.

Then what? What had him thinking life on the road was better than life with Maisey Clark and her baby and his dog and his siblings and their children and this peaceful place full of his family history?

Million-dollar question.

Chapter Thirteen

At 8:45 the next morning, Maisey stepped out of her cabin, Chloe in her chest carrier, to head to the Kid Zone when she stopped and stared all around her. Had a bunch of elves secretly spread their Christmas dust in the night to make the ranch more festive? Even at this hour when the twinkling white and multicolored lights weren't even on, the whole place felt so utterly magical, like a Christmas village. The Dawsons had really gone all out for the fair, decorating the place to the holiday nines. The streetlamps were wrapped with alternating red and green tinsel, and more wreaths had been hung with bright red bows on the barns.

There were white lights lining the outside posts of the pastures, which would be lit up come dusk.

"Merry Christmas," Angie, one of chef Cowboy Joe's assistant cooks, called as she turned up the path toward the cafeteria. The woman waved, a Santa hat on her head, green-and-red-striped tights under her long blue down coat.

"Merry Christmas!" Maisey called back with a smile.

There were a lot of holiday greetings going on, the staffers, also in their Santa hats, heading to their posts and special assignments for the fair, excited for the gates to open and visitors to start pouring in.

"Oh, Chloe, look," Maisey said, pointing across the path at the rescued reindeer pasture. Two of the reindeer were staring right at her and Chloe with their sweet faces, their antlers high and huge. "It's like they're saying 'Merry Christmas' to us, too," she told the baby. "Your grandma and grandpa would have loved those reindeer," she added on a whisper. As soon as those words were out, she realized she wasn't overtaken by the usual fleeting sadness. The thought of her parents felt rich and warm, like a comforting hug. *She* felt…full of anticipation, *happy*.

She stopped walking and gasped. "It's back,"

she whispered to Chloe. "My Christmas spirit! It's back!"

The red and green, the beautifully decorated trees, the wreaths, the signs for Santa's hut in the lodge—nothing she saw right now made her feel sad or reminded her of her losses. Where she once had a hole was now filled in with only the slightest tinge of bittersweet—remembrance versus sadness. Christmas was in her heart, in the air, all around her.

She wasn't even sure if Rex Dawson had given her back the holiday; Maisey had let it in. She'd opened up to it. He'd helped, definitely. He'd been like her own private Santa, bringing his cheer and his goodness. But Maisey hadn't been closed off, just as she hadn't been closed off to Rex. It was how she'd fallen for him. And no matter what happened between them, she was happy she had fallen. Love, for the best reasons, was a good thing, not something to hide from like she'd been doing since her ex had betrayed her.

Inside the lodge, Maisey looked at the Christmas tree at the end of the hall near the grand stairs as she did every morning and every night, and there was no wistfulness, no emptiness—just warmth. Her past was just *part* of her; it no longer consumed her.

You started this, Rex Dawson, so thank you. I

might have finished it, but you set me on the path to Christmas. If I never see you again after the twenty-sixth, I'll never forget what you did for me.

As Maisey headed into the Kid Zone, she knew today would be atypical. The guests and their kids would attend the fair, and if someone needed a breather or wanted to practice a song, they could always come hang out here, where there were a few activity tables set up to make last-minute gifts out of pine cones and Popsicle sticks and pom-poms and stickers. She wasn't expecting more than a third of the usual crew, probably mainly the Dawsons' kids since their parents were all working the fair in various ways.

As the clock struck nine, all the Dawson parents had dropped off their little ones. The only Dawson she hadn't seen this morning was Rex, but she was sure he'd be in, at some point, to double-check that everything was ready for tonight's big performance.

Like right now. Her heart gave a little leap as he came through the door. He took off his jacket and scarf on the way over to her, and despite the early hour, she was struck by how sexy he was.

"How is one of my favorite babies?" he asked Chloe in the carrier on her chest. He covered his handsome face and opened up his hands for peekaboo.

Chloe gurgled.

"Rex, just tell me why you've been avoiding me," Maisey blurted out. *Whoa.* She hadn't even planned on confronting him. But she was glad she had. The only way to get answers was to ask questions. "We've gotten too close for this or for you to not be honest. Just say it."

He put his hands down and looked right at Maisey, his expression contrite. "I'm sorry for that. I'm just trying to figure some things out."

She put her hands on her hips. "And so you have to be all distant to do that?"

"Actually, yes. Because you're one of the things I need to figure out, Maisey."

He loves you, too, she knew with sudden clarity. Or her newfound Christmas cheer was upping her confidence. *And it's messing with his plans— and what he thought he wanted for himself.*

"I thought you already knew where we stood," she said. "Nowhere. You're leaving in three days, remember?"

He reached up a hand to briefly touch her face. "If I want to pretend there's nothing between us, sure. But there's a lot between us. More than I ever thought could be."

Finally. At least she knew she was right. He did love her. But he was torn between their very unexpected romance and being a man who never made commitments, never stuck around.

"And that doesn't mesh with your plans," she said.

"It doesn't mesh with my *life*, Maisey. I'm due back to my job on the twenty-sixth. This isn't about me jet-setting around. It's my work. It's everything I am."

He'd said that last part kind of slowly as if maybe he was realizing being a US marshal wasn't everything he was, just a part. Just as his family was a part of him, and this ranch.

And hopefully her.

This conversation had her thinking there was a chance for them. But if she let herself hope, what if she got dashed? She could very easily not come first here. If the fear—if that was what it was— that had him gripped about commitment won out, she'd lose him. She'd been so prepared for him to walk out of her life. But that was before she knew there was a possibility that he'd stay because he *did* have feelings for her.

She wished she knew what to say, the magic words to change his mind, change his cells. She needed that elf dust. She could tell him she'd gotten her Christmas spirit back, but that would be reason for him to leave. Mission accomplished.

Anyway, he'd seen her slowly take the holiday back for herself. Rex didn't miss anything.

"I'm all set for the Santa hut to open at ten. I'll be in there for two-hour intervals till three o'clock. Then I'll be back here to help out with showtime."

"You're going to be a great Santa. I can attest to that."

Even if I'm not going to get what I want from you, Rex Dawson.

Before he could respond, the door opened again, and the eight-year-old Caletti twins came in looking miserable. Their parents stood by the check-in, their expressions worried.

"Uh-oh," Maisey whispered. "I see teary eyes and sad faces. Let me go see what's wrong."

Maisey walked over to them, aware of Rex heading nearby to the chair where he'd put his jacket and tool kit. She could *feel* him ready to pay attention, to listen in. He wanted to see if he could help, she knew. To "serve and protect" was so ingrained in him.

But that didn't mean he had to fight injustice and chase down fugitives across the state, across the country. He could serve and protect right here in Bear Ridge. If he wanted.

"Hey, girls," Maisey said. "Why the sad faces?" The flame-haired twins were usually so animated, added to by their colorful dresses and striped tights and light-up sneakers. When they were down, everyone always noticed.

"We can't remember any of the words to 'Rudolph the Red-Nosed Reindeer,'" Ava said, panic in her voice.

Amelia nodded, her eyes glistening. "Especially our solo part, when we get to take a step forward and it's just us two singing that one line."

"Well, you definitely know the first line," Maisey pointed out, "because you already said it! It's the name of the song itself!"

The twins brightened a bit. "Oh, yeah!" they said in unison.

Maisey turned to their parents. "Why don't you check in about a half hour. They'll have the song down and you all can enjoy the fair together."

The parents smiled with relief and left.

Chloe let out a wail, and Rex put a hand on Maisey's shoulder. "I've got Chloe. You handle song duty. I don't even know all the words to 'Rudolph' and I've been listening to practice for days."

"Thanks, Rex." *You are the best*, she thought. *So you can't leave in three days and come visit every few months. Stay, stay, stay.*

"Even a grown-up doesn't know the words!" Ava said, a smile finally on her face.

Rex plucked Chloe out of the carrier on Maisey's

chest, standing so tantalizingly close. She liked the scent of his shampoo. The way his dark lashes lay on his cheeks as he looked down at Chloe. His incredible shoulders in that navy Henley. The way his jeans molded to his body. Even his scuffed brown leather cowboy boots were sexy.

As she took the carrier off and set it on a chair, she watched him hold her baby girl against his chest. He headed over to the big window where the reindeer pasture was visible, narrating everything he was going to do: wave hi to the reindeer, tell her why some reindeer had antlers in the winter and some didn't, sing one of the holiday songs that he was sure he'd mess up and show her the tree that would soon have the kids' gifts under it.

Stay, she thought again. *Mischievous elves, get to work on him.* That was the thing about getting back her Christmas spirit. She believed in magic again. And she wasn't above asking for a little holiday help.

"Maisey, Chloe is really cute," Ava Caletti said.

"Supercute," Amelia added. "Does she look like you or Rex more?"

Maisey almost choked. They thought Rex was Chloe's dad? The baby didn't look anything like Rex—she was blond like Maisey with huge hazel eyes that were turning darker and would probably be pale brown like her mom's. Maisey was grateful she did look so much like her and not her biological father.

She froze at the realization that she'd referred to her ex that way. Biological. Because she was ready for a good man to become Maisey's daddy.

And she wished that man could be Rex.

"Rex isn't Chloe's dad," Maisey said, the words like cold water on her head. "He's a very good family friend. And a Dawson. His family own this ranch." She pointed to a sign on the door with the ranch's name and logo.

"Oh, we thought he was Chloe's father," Ava said.

Amelia nodded. "Yeah, he's always taking care of her like dads do. See?" she added, pointing.

Maisey glanced at where Rex was sitting down on an alphabet rug in the baby/toddler section, Chloe sitting beside him and batting at the little dangly bunny he was holding in front of her. A huge laugh came from her, Maisey's favorite sound, rivaled only by the kids singing their holiday songs.

He's good with Chloe because he loves Chloe, too. He loves us. He just either doesn't realize it yet or can't compute. He might need some time. Or he'll just take off on the twenty-sixth as planned and push all the stuff that had been bothering him away. Such as his ambivalence. His unfinished business with his father. Just leave it all behind here.

She hoped he didn't do that.

"Hey, girls," she said, needing to change the subject, "why don't we practice right on the stage? Just the two of you. Let's go!"

The girls grinned and raced over onto the stage. Maisey got out the song sheet and handed each girl a copy, and they sang it while reading. Then she asked them to try it without the sheet. Then one more time.

Perfection. They stepped forward during their solo and got it just right.

Maisey clapped, and Rex stood up and gave his own standing ovation, then scooped up Chloe and walked over. "Girls, you've got this. You know the song inside out."

"Yay, thanks, Maisey," they said in unison with grins, and they ran off to the clubhouse on the far side of the room.

Rex stood beside her, shifting Chloe in his arms. "You're really good at your job. You're good at being a person."

"That's probably my favorite compliment ever." She tried to smile, but she was too touched and didn't want to get all emotional on him. "Turns out the girls did know the song and just got a little stage fright over breakfast when they sang it for their parents."

His phone pinged with a text, and he checked it. "I have to get going. Noah and Axel could use an extra pair of eyes on the various paths and the tables. Daisy's already said that all the families already booked stays for next Christmas. And all the cabins are already booked through next summer and there's a waiting list for cancellations."

"Wow. That's great. I feel like I have serious job security now."

"I know for a fact that Daisy thinks you're doing an amazing job. You'd have security without the ranch being the sudden hot spot of Wyoming. Maybe even the West."

Good. I need this job, this place. With or without you. But the thought of being here without him suddenly seemed unimaginable. He *was* the Dawson Family Guest Ranch. "Thanks for watching Chloe for me. She sure does adore you."

She really hadn't meant to say it. But it was true and just came out.

"It's mutual," he said. He handed her over to Maisey, gave the baby's head a little caress, shot Maisey a brief smile and then headed out.

She watched the door for a few seconds, wishing he'd come back. How could she already miss him?

"What am I gonna do, Chloe?" she whispered.

And then, "Right now, let's go check on Annabel and Chance."

The twins were still sleeping. Danny was playing his favorite superhero game with Hannah by the nap cave, flying his stuffed caped lion overhead while she had an action figure who needed Super Zul's help. Sadie had told her that the lion was named Zul after Axel, who was Danny's hero, but he hadn't been able to pronounce Axel's name when they first met. Axel, then a search-and-rescue worker, had been the one to find missing Danny on a family trip up Clover Mountain—and had fallen in love with Sadie, Danny's mother. If Rex stuck around, she had no doubt he'd be Chloe's hero—after Super Mommy, of course.

The rest of the day passed slowly. Every now and then, she'd be drawn to the window, showing Chloe the smiling guests passing by, marveling at the decorations and the activities and the reindeer. On her lunch break, she'd fortified herself with a delicious chicken burrito and she'd swiped a cup of eggnog to go. A few more kids came in and out of the Kid Zone, wanting to work on their songs, but otherwise she was able to keep a tight rein on the ready-for-showtime stage area, no crumpled hoodies lying around, no smashed pretzels on any of the chairs.

At 4:15, the parents all dropped off their kids

so that they could get into costume, do any last-minute practices, work out any stage fright and get into places. The parents would be back at 4:45 to take their seats and get their programs, which Maisey had created with her boss's laptop and printer. Her two staffers were here to help get the little kids changed. Everything was ready.

Showtime, she said to herself with a little flourish, and it occurred to her that she'd been so busy the past hour that she hadn't even thought about Rex. Maybe that was the ticket—stay superbusy. Of course, the least busy day of the year would be December 26. When he'd be saying goodbye.

Rex had been fully prepared for tears, meltdowns and demands in the Santa hut, but all the kids who'd visited were excited and launched into lists of dream gifts, from Lego sets, to iPhones, to Barbies, to action figures, to a trip to Disneyland. The Caletti twins wanted a reindeer. Zara, whom Rex had expected to talk about her late parents, excitedly asked for voice lessons and had said that Emily and Ethan had already talked to Santa about it but she wanted to remind him. Axel and Sadie had come in with Danny, who didn't quite understand what was going on. All he wanted for Christmas was to fly his superhero lion. That one was easy-peasy. When they'd left, Axel had whispered, "Santa. You never cease to surprise me, Rex," and shot him a thumbs-up, his son in his arms.

Now Rex stood in the curtained "side stage" area from where the kids would make their grand entrance. He was serving as an extra pair of eyes as the two Kid Zone staffers were busy with last-minute buttoning and zipping and soothing worries. He could hear sniffling coming from somewhere and peered around heads.

Uh-oh. Zara, in her really cute elf costume, was suddenly crying.

Maisey was at the door, welcoming parents and handing out programs. He was relieved to see her come "backstage," and he upped his chin at Zara.

Maisey hurried over to Zara and led her away from the group, then knelt in front of her. "Hey, what's wrong, sweetie?"

Tears ran down her face. "My mom and dad aren't here. Emily and Ethan aren't my real mom and dad. I just wish my parents could be here and see me singing onstage."

"I know you're sad about that, Zara. Emily and Ethan love you and care about you and they're here to cheer you on. Ethan even has the video app on his phone ready to record the whole show."

Rex had to hand it to Maisey. She really was spectacular at her job. She gave everyone her full attention no matter what, and right now, with a show about to start, Zara needed her and that was that.

Zara shrugged and wiped her hands under her eyes. "Don't you wish your parents were here?"

"Yes. I do. But you know where they are?"

"Heaven?"

"Heaven and also right here," Maisey said, putting her hand against her chest. "They're always with me."

Zara put her hand to her heart and her chin to her chest to get a look. "They're in here?"

Rex wondered if his dad was in his heart. He didn't feel Bo Dawson there, not that he'd know what that would feel like. But Maisey clearly did, so it had to be real, something you *felt*, were aware of when you really needed to be, something that comforted.

Maisey nodded. "I know it. They're always with you, always watching over you. And something else I'm sure of? They're so glad to know that the Harwoods love you so much and take such good care of you. Because that's what parents do, right?"

Zara sniffled. "Yeah."

"Sometimes something good comes from something bad, Zara. I think Emily and Ethan are something really good."

Aww, Maisey. You knocked it out of the park. She's the best, plain and simple.

"I do like my dog, Poppy," Zara said, her face brightening. "I never had a dog before. And we have a huge fish tank, too, and I got to name all of them except one who Emily named a long time ago. And Emily always brushes my hair every morning and everyone always says they like my hair. And Ethan lets me walk Poppy every night after dinner while he wears this really nerdy hat with a searchlight on it. And I told Emily that I really, really, really want voice lessons for Christmas and she said she'd talk to Santa. I told him about it today in the Santa hut."

Maisey smiled. "Santa's awesome. And Emily and Ethan are sitting in the audience right now, waiting to watch you sing."

"I can't wait for my solo," Zara said.

Maisey gave her a big hug. "It's just about time to go out onstage. Ready?"

Zara nodded firmly, her brown eyes clear. "Ready!"

Rex caught Maisey's eye and flashed her an inadequate thumbs-up for how moving that was to watch and listen to.

She smiled back, and for the millionth time he wondered how he'd deal with not seeing that beautiful face every day.

"Okay, kids," she said to the group. "I'm going to go out there and introduce the show. After you hear me say, 'And now I'm proud to present the children's holiday show,' you'll walk out in the order we practiced and take your places. Hannah will help direct you."

The kids were practically bouncing up and down with excitement.

Rex peered out of the curtain to see all the Dawsons in the first two rows. He took the seat Ford had saved him between him and one of the parents.

"Nice of you and Zeke to come," Rex said.

"Would we miss our nephew's first annual children's holiday show debut? No way." He glanced at Rex and leaned a bit closer.

Rex pulled the yellow pocket watch from inside his jacket and stared down at it. He'd been carrying it around since he'd found it. The letter was inside his wallet, and he hadn't reread that, but every time he flipped open the plastic cover of the watch and looked at that goofy cartoon seahorse—*It's time for fun!*—he smiled.

"Gave you some closure?" Ford asked, his eyes on the watch.

Rex shrugged. "This might be a little heavy for right now," he whispered, "but let me ask you something. You think you're a cop to chase ghosts?"

"I think it gets mixed in there, yeah. I feel like it's time to stop. I want something else, Rex."

"What, though? Besides small-town life and less crime."

Ford glanced at him. "Family. I want to get married."

Rex stared at his eldest brother, truly shocked. "Someone check the sky for flying pigs." He sat back for a moment. "Wow."

"I'm ready. Now I just have to find my wife."

My wife. My wife. My wife. Those were two words that still didn't seem to work together for him. *My* and *wife.*

Maisey came out onstage, and his chest rumbled.

"It can get too late, Rex," Ford whispered. "Everyone knows that. Don't get to that point."

Before Rex could ask what he meant, not that he was sure he wanted to know, Maisey welcomed the crowd and introduced the show, and the kids came out to thunderous applause, including his own. Noah and Zeke both let out a wolf whistle.

The kids were lined up in their places and the music started. Annalise stepped forward and introduced the first song, "Frosty the Snowman."

"I still prefer 'Frotty Noman,'" Axel whispered, turning around from his seat in front of them.

Rex smiled. So did he. He'd miss that. And these kids. This place. He clapped and cheered after each song, from "A Holly Jolly Christmas" to "Rudolph the Red-Nosed Reindeer" to "All I Want for Christmas Is My Two Front Teeth," the audience roaring when seven-year-old Kyra Lopez stepped forward in her reindeer costume and smiled superwide where her two front teeth were missing in a mouth full of baby teeth.

A half hour later, the show was over, and everyone jumped to their feet, giving the kids a standing ovation. Rex glanced over at Maisey, who joined the kids onstage for their final bow. Then she handed each child their wrapped gift to very excited faces and dismissed the group to their families.

Zara ran over to Emily and hugged her, then did the same to Ethan. "I was in my first show! Did you get it on video?"

Ethan nodded, and Rex could see how emotional the man was. "I sure did. You were so awesome, Z."

"Yay, thank you!" she said, hugging him again.

"And guess what's the special for dinner at the caf," Emily added. "Mac and cheese in special honor of the great job you all did. You really were amazing, Zara. You sang your solo so beautifully. We're both so proud of you."

Zara beamed and reached a hand up to her heart, and Rex, who wasn't the biggest softy out there or even among his siblings, almost lost it. He did feel people in that steel-cased chest of his. His mom. His siblings. His niece and nephews. Maisey and Chloe. Even the Dawson Family Guest Ranch was in his heart. But he didn't feel his dad in there. What did that mean? No way could he ask Ford *that*. Daisy, maybe. She could psychoanalyze it for a good hour.

He glanced at Maisey and saw her watching Zara with her parents, her eyes glistening, her hand on her own heart.

She did have *his*, that was for sure.

My wife, my wife, my wife.

Suddenly his head felt stuffed with cotton. His collar was tightening. His skin was itchy. Those words didn't apply to him because his life wasn't set up to accommodate a wife. Or a family. Or a dog, which was why he'd have to leave River with Daisy. He let his head drop back with a hard sigh as he tugged at his collar. Was it hot in here?

"You all right?" Ford asked.

"Just need some air," he said, getting up and heading out.

He had no doubt Maisey watched him leave,

which made him feel worse. He should be congratulating her, high-fiving the brave and talented kids, putting his nephew, who'd made his stage debut tonight, on his shoulders. Instead, he was outside in front of the lodge gulping cold air, and he'd forgotten his jacket, so he was freezing to boot.

"Dude, terrible advice," a voice said.

Rex looked left. Tyler was sulkily walking over to him. Oh, damn. Had he messed that up, too?

"Right after the show ended, I asked Annalise if I could talk to her for a sec. Fine, she says. So I bring her over behind the curtain and tell her I really like her and can we have a long-distance relationship and text and stuff. And you know what she said?"

Rex had a feeling.

Tyler frowned. "She said she liked me like a little brother. Hello? What? I'm not seven! We're just a year apart."

"Sorry, Tyler. I know you liked her a lot and hoped to stay in touch."

"Now I feel stupid. I made a total moron of myself. She'll tell all her friends about the idiot eighth grader who asked her to be his girlfriend—long-distance, too."

"Nope. I think you made her feel good. You gave her a big compliment."

"How?" Tyler asked. "I'm seven, remember? That kid brother."

Rex smiled and shook his head. "You two are friends, right? She does like you. And when someone you like likes you back, even more romantically than you feel, it's a compliment. I'm sure she's very touched, Tyler."

"Maybe we can stay in touch as just friends?" he said.

"I'll bet she'll go for that."

"I take back what I said about the bad advice. In it to win it, right? Even the great Kobe Bryant missed a basket or two. I'm gonna go ask someone to take a pic of us to remember her by. Later, dude. I guess it's better to be friend-zoned than ghosted, right?"

He'd friend-zoned Maisey and now he was going to ghost her. Well, not really. He'd call. He'd text. That meant he wasn't really disappearing from her life.

Tyler ran back inside. Rex was right behind because he was so cold. But Maisey came out with his jacket.

She handed it to him and he gratefully put it on. "I happened to glance out the window and saw you talking to Tyler in just your shirt. I could see you shivering."

"Ah, much better," he said, zipping up to his chin. "Thank you."

Friend-zone. Ghosted. Leaving but texting every week or so: How are you, how's Chloe? That felt so...lacking.

All he knew for sure was that he had to leave, had to get back to his life.

But not before he gave her the Christmas she deserved. He could tell that Maisey had gotten back her Christmas spirit. He saw it in every-thing she did. The way she gazed with wonder at the reindeer, at the Christmas tree in the Kid Zone, the smile that lit up her face as the kids had sung their holiday songs. He had no idea why that didn't make him feel as good as he'd thought it would, that he could leave easier.

"So, Maisey, I was hoping to come by for a while tomorrow night for Christmas Eve. I have some gifts for you and Chloe and Snowbell."

She grinned. "The three of us never turn down gifts. Well, maybe Snowbell does if it's not catnip related." She smiled and held his gaze for a sec-ond. "I have something for you, too."

"You didn't have to get me anything," he said. "But thank you."

Her smile struck him as wistful, conflicted, and he wanted to pull her into a hug and just hold her. But he stayed put.

"Does seven work?" he asked. "I plan to bring dinner, so don't eat."

"Presents and dinner? I could get used to that," she said, then looked away before pasting a bright smile on her beautiful face. "Seven is perfect. Chloe will be up for a good half hour so she can be part of the celebration."

I wish you could get used to it. You should have presents and dinner and everything your heart desires every single day.

He wanted to reach out and hug her so bad. But he stuffed his hands in his pockets. He'd see her tomorrow night, give her the great Christmas he'd planned to, from dinner to gifts, and then he'd feel okay about leaving the day after Christmas. He was sure then he'd get that closure he'd been after when it came to Maisey Clark.

So why did he feel so crummy?

Chapter Fourteen

The next day, Christmas Eve, Maisey's doorbell rang at six thirty, a little too early for Rex, but maybe he'd been so unable to wait another minute to be near her that he was early.

Suuurrre. She smiled at her ridiculousness and pulled open the door. It was Daisy, carrying a bright red bag with green ribbons twirling from the handles.

Her boss, wearing adorable Mrs. Claus dangling earrings, held up the bag. "Just a little something to say not only 'Merry Christmas,' but to thank you for all your incredible work pulling together the kids' show. It was absolutely great.

Even my two-year-old nephew was singing and shaking his little hips."

Maisey grinned and held the door wide for Daisy to come inside. "I loved working with the kids. But I can't take full credit. Your brother was a huge help. Honestly, I couldn't have done it without him. He watched Chloe when she was fussy, he took me shopping, he built the stage and sets, he made me feel like I could do anything—even put together a kids' holiday show in less than five days."

He really did make her feel like she could do anything.

"My brothers and I have all been in total shock this past week, Maisey. Seeing Rex holding a baby he's not related to? Going shopping for kiddie costumes? Painting pieces of wood for a show? Being Santa?"

Maisey smiled. "That all sounds very much like the Rex I know."

"Ha, yeah, because he's *changed*. You've changed him."

She felt tears prick the backs of her eyes and willed herself not to cry. "Nope. I didn't. Or he wouldn't be leaving the day after tomorrow."

Daisy put the bag down and reached out to squeeze Maisey's hand. "Maybe he won't."

"Nah, he will. Is. He told me so just yesterday. He's told me just about every day that I've known him."

"Because he *thinks* he's leaving. Leaving is what he does. But that was before you came into his life."

"I want to believe that. But when someone tells you their plans outright, it's wise to listen. I thought I could save myself the heartache by focusing on the fact that he's in my life temporarily. But nope—heartbreak city."

Daisy gave her a gentle smile. "Yeah, I know how that feels. Look, maybe he will leave like he's been saying. But I wouldn't give up on him just yet. It's not the twenty-sixth. He hasn't tried walking away from the woman he loves—and we all know he loves you. Nothing is more obvious to the five of us. And I'd like to see him try to leave this precious baby," she added, picking up her bag and walking over to Chloe in her baby swing in the small living room.

Rex did seem attached to Chloe. But he also seemed attached to his baby relatives—family— and he easily came and went from their lives.

Just as he would go from Maisey and Chloe's.

Daisy put her shopping bag down again and reached into it. "For you, sweet Chloe." She took out three sets of warm pj's, a board book with chewable edges, three pacifiers, a hair bow, five pairs of adorable socks and one of those little toy license plates with her name on it.

These Dawsons, Maisey thought, so touched she couldn't speak for a second. They were truly the best people she knew.

"Oh, Daisy, this is just too generous. I can't thank you enough. I have something for you, too. Just a little something." She reached into the little door on the console table and pulled out a wrapped gift.

She watched Daisy open it, her blue eyes lighting up at the sight of the mug with World's Best Boss across it, two candy canes below it. "You really are, Daisy." The mug wasn't much or expensive, but she knew Daisy would like it.

"I love this more than you will ever know. Thank you." Her boss gave her a big hug. "And this is for you," she said, reaching into the bag for a big wrapped box. "Kind of a hodgepodge of stuff I thought you'd like. I'm a hodgepodger."

Maisey grinned and opened the box. A gift certificate to the steak house in town. Yum. A beautiful dark red mohair sweater that she absolutely loved. Pink wool socks with sparkly bits. And something that brought tears to her eyes. A framed sign that read Maisey Clark, Dawson Family Guest Ranch Staffer of the Season Award. *You Rock* was written below.

"You're gonna make me cry before Rex comes and then I'll have mascara running down my face. Daisy, thank you so much. For everything."

"You are very welcome. Oh, one more thing." Daisy pulled over a chair, reached into her magic red bag again and pulled out a sprig of mistletoe, then stood on the chair. "Conveniently already has double-sided tape applied." She grinned and pasted it above the door frame.

Maisey hugged her again. As she closed the door behind Daisy, she glanced up at the mistletoe, not sure how much good it would do her. Or them.

Rex might have gone a little overboard with gifts for Maisey and Chloe. He put down the two big shopping bags and rang the bell at Maisey's cabin. When she opened the door, he almost gasped. Maisey wasn't in her usual jeans or leggings or long sweaters. She wore a slinky sleeveless red dress and black high heels. A tantalizing hint of her spicy-flowery perfume got him as he closed the door and set down the bags.

"Christmas Eve," she said. "Had to dress up."

He was glad he had, too—in dark gray wool pants and a black sweater. To stop staring at her, he looked over at Chloe, who was decked out in a red velvet dress and adorable polka-dot stretchy pants, a green headband with a bow in her hair.

"You look very festive, Chloe," he told the baby, kneeling down in front of her and giving her cheek a caress. The doorbell rang and Rex stood up with a sly smile. "You might want to get that, Maisey."

She eyed him with a quizzical smile and opened the door. Two people with Bear Ridge Caterers on their white chef coats wheeled in a cart with several lidded platters and bowls. "What is all this?"

"I said I was bringing dinner. Not that I was making dinner. I left that to the pros. Trust me, you don't want *my* attempt at filet mignon in peppercorn sauce with all the trimmings. Everything would be either burned or half-raw." He signed the receipt from the caterers and they left, his stomach rumbling from how good everything smelled.

"I've never had a catered dinner before," she said. "Not even at my wedding. That was a barbecue with a choice of hot dogs or hamburgers."

Something told him that wasn't the wedding reception she'd dreamed about. Though, knowing Maisey, she probably only cared about the groom, not the trappings. He pictured her sitting at a patio table, eating a hot dog and trying to not drip mustard on her gown. If she'd even worn a gown. "You can never go wrong with a grilled hot dog or hamburger."

"Facts—as Tyler and Annalise would say. I've learned lots of new teen slang and lingo this past week."

He laughed. "Me, too, just from a couple hours the past few days of working on the sets with them. Did you know Tyler has a mad crush on Annalise? I counseled him to tell her how he feels. I hope I got it right."

"Asking is everything. You don't ask, you don't get. I'm all for self-advocating."

"Good. I haven't gotten up to teenagers yet with my niece and nephews, so I had no idea if I was giving him good advice."

"You definitely did," she said, and he forced himself not to let his gaze wander up and down that sexy red dress.

"Shall we?" he asked. "I'll wheel the cart into the kitchen and you can bring in Chloe. I wish she was at the steak stage so she could enjoy this incredible dinner."

Maisey grinned. "She's already had her beloved butternut squash baby food, but she can have her milk while we eat."

In the small kitchen, he put the cart next to the table and transferred the platters, the steaks, drenched in béarnaise sauce and dotted with peppercorns, making his mouth water. There was garlic-tinged asparagus and rosemary roast potatoes, plus French bread and a green salad in a miso-something dressing that managed to smell delicious. He put the tiramisu for dessert in the refrigerator.

Maisey reached into a cabinet and brought out plates and silverware and began setting the table. "I have a bottle of red wine that the Kid Zone staffers gave me for Christmas. Want a glass with dinner?"

"Definitely." He wheeled the cart over by the door. When he came back, Maisey had put the wine and glasses on the table along with a corkscrew and had given Chloe her milk.

"She's started to hold her own bottle," Maisey said, her gaze tender on her daughter. "These little milestones blow me away. Every month, every few weeks, really, it's something new and amazing."

"Her eyes are turning light brown like yours," he said, looking from Chloe to Maisey and back. "She's going to be your mini-me."

"I won't lie. I'm glad she looks like me and not her father."

He opened the bottle of wine and poured. "Think he'll ever come back to see her?" He wanted to know, but did he have to bring that up on Christmas

Eve? He wished he could take it back. Maisey didn't need to be thinking about that right now. He held up a hand. "I shouldn't have asked. Forget I did." He handed her the glass of wine, then held his up.

She clinked. "Merry Christmas, Rex."

"Merry Christmas."

She took a small sip. "I'm glad you asked, actually. About her dad. It's true that I don't love talking about all that, but it's not good to pretend the hard stuff doesn't exist. Plus, if you don't talk about these things, get them out in the open and explored, they fester. That just makes everything worse."

He sipped the wine and realized he was a master at that. Pretending. Sweeping under the ole rug. But he was also a master at not letting the ugliness in his past get to him, let alone fester.

Or was he kidding himself? He'd shut his father out of his heart, hadn't he? Rex mentally shrugged, unsure of any of this. He'd like to think he knew himself pretty well, was self-aware. But when it came to his dad, the memories, the loss—that kiddie pocket watch and letter—and Rex didn't know the first thing about how he really felt. Bo Dawson "stuff" had been long blocked by an impenetrable wall.

This was what he got for asking her a too-personal question. An unexpected perusal of his own head. He reached for the platter of steaks and slid it closer to her.

Her eyes lit up as she took a steak and spooned the incredible sauce over it. He did the same, and as they filled their plates with salad and asparagus and potatoes, he was relieved not to be thinking.

"I don't think we'll be seeing Chloe's father again," she said, about to cut into her steak. "When I told him I was pregnant, he said he doubted the baby was his. He told his family I cheated and that 'the kid' wasn't his. Then when he left me, his family turned on me, too, and said they were done with me. I didn't have much contact with them, anyway, but that was the last I've heard from them." She took a bite of her steak, sitting back for a moment to appreciate it. "This is amazing. To be honest, Rex, I've never had filet mignon."

He reached across the table and covered her hand with his, then lifted his glass again.

She smiled and picked up hers. "To good firsts, then."

"Very good firsts." They clinked and sipped and resumed eating, the steak incredible, the side dishes popping with flavor.

"I didn't ever cheat, by the way," she added, forking a roast potato. "All I wanted back then was a husband, a family. I'd never do anything to jeopardize it, even if the marriage needed a ton of work."

She'd already lived a lifetime in twenty-three years. Loss and hardship and a jerk of an ex-husband. But a beautiful, healthy baby, a great job she loved and true friends who'd do anything for her—his entire family. Plus him.

"Sounds like you really tried," he said, "longer and harder than anyone could deal with."

"I'm ready for cheerier subjects. It's Christmas Eve and a time for festivity and celebrating."

Rex smiled, appreciating her attitude, which was always so positive. He could learn a lot from her. "I'm glad you're enjoying dinner. My brothers and I hired these caterers to whip up a month's worth of meals for Daisy when Tony was born. She raved about the food. So did Harrison when they finally got together as a couple."

"What a great gift. You should know, Daisy put some mistletoe above the door. Your sister is still hoping to get you paired up and staying for good."

"Nah, she'll move on to Ford now he's set on moving back to Bear Ridge and joining the police force here. He told me he's ready to settle down. Wants a wife and kids, the whole thing."

Maisey glanced at him. "Wow. Daisy will be thrilled. That'll be three brothers with only two to go. Or one, since you're—" She stopped talking and cut into her steak.

"I'm what?" he asked. Did he want to know, though?

"I was going to say 'a lost cause' on the subject. But, oh heck, I'm just going to say it. I keep hoping that's not true."

Chloe let out a fussy wail, saving the day. Well, saving him from having to respond when he had no idea what to say. He wanted to stay *and* leave. Something was clearly at war in his head and body. Maybe all that "hard stuff" he had pushed under the rug for years.

"What's the matter, sweetie?" Maisey asked, taking the bottle, but Chloe grabbed it back. She laughed. "Sor-*ry*! Are we leaving you out of the conversation? Is that the issue?" She glanced at Rex, and he knew she was giving him the out. Which he'd take.

They got through the rest of dinner talking about the show and the kids and how she was sure the Harwoods were on their way to good things. He told funny stories about his siblings. She told him what seemed like funny stories about the old trailer she'd lived in, but he hated the idea of her in that run-down place, alone with an infant and worrying how she'd pay her bills.

He forked his last potato, which practically

melted in his mouth with rosemary and chives. He wanted her to eat like this every night. He wanted her not just safe, not just secure, but truly comfortable.

"You know, Maisey, my condo in Cheyenne is really nicely decorated, thanks to the interior designer I hired while I was on the road. I'm never there to enjoy any of it. Why don't I have the furniture shipped here? You could trade that lumpy plaid couch for a plush memory-foam sofa that you'll never want to get up from. Lamps, artwork, tables with great craftsmanship, gorgeous rugs. All yours. Just say the word."

She stared at him for a second. "No, thanks. I'm fine with lumps. That's what I can afford right now. If this cabin hadn't come semifurnished, I'd be sitting on a box with a cushion on it."

"Which is why you should let me ship my furniture." He didn't need any of that stuff. He couldn't even remember the last time he was in that place.

It didn't escape his attention that he didn't think of it as *home*. It wasn't.

She shook her head. "If you want to share your stuff with me, Rex, include yourself. If not, I'll take care of myself."

He felt his face burn. This conversation hadn't gone like he'd hoped. "I just meant—"

"I know what you meant. And I know you mean well. I'm hardly an all-or-nothing person— I *know* I could use help. I *know* I need things for the cabin. But I'll get there. Your fancy, expensive furniture won't fit right in this cozy place, anyway. And I don't mean proportionally. The cabin is about home and comfort and second chances. Not a decorator making choices and spending tens of thousands on furnishings you didn't even select yourself and never use. You know?"

He supposed so. *But I want to give you everything.* If she could read his mind right now, she'd say: *Hardly. You're not including yourself.*

He nodded. "I hear you. I'll get these plates out of the way." He stood up and began piling empty platters on top of one another. "Those guys will be back in about an hour to pick up the cart." He glanced at Chloe, who let out a big yawn. "Oh, I'd better give her her gifts before she has to skedaddle off to bed."

Maisey smiled and stood, too. "It's definitely late for her. But tonight is special. It's Christmas Eve. Before you came into my life, I would be staring out the window, all conflicted. Now I just feel filled up. I've always been a blessings counter, but it's more than that. I'm happy, Rex."

Before he knew what he was doing, he leaned forward and kissed her on the lips, his hands on either side of her face. He pulled away just slightly, looking at her flushed cheeks, her flashing eyes. "I know you are. At least I'll have that."

She stepped back, and he knew he'd said the wrong thing. *Done* the wrong thing.

"I shouldn't have kissed you," he said. "I'm sorry. I—"

She held up a hand. "I'm glad you did. Especially because there was no mistletoe over our heads. It wasn't a *had to* kiss. It was a *want to*."

He smiled and wished he could kiss her again and again and again.

"I'll load up the dishes." She began stacking plates and silverware, very obviously not looking at him.

Maisey Clark, Maisey Clark, Maisey Clark. Her name echoed in his head. Maybe this was what happened when you cared deeply about someone before you'd ever met them, before you even knew how spectacularly beautiful and kind and strong they were.

The cart was ready to go, and grateful for the distraction, he moved it by the front door, and they headed into the living room. Rex pulled all the gifts from the bags and set them under the tree.

"Oh, look, who is this for?" he asked Chloe, holding up a big pink-wrapped box.

Maisey sat down on the rug in front of the tree, Chloe on her lap, and shook her head with a grin. "You do realize she's six months old. How many gifts did you get her?"

He sat down beside Maisey. "One for every month she's been alive."

She laughed and took the pink box. She unwrapped it, holding up the yellow blanket bordered by pastel animals of every kind. She put it against her face. "So soft. And her name is embroidered on it," she added, reaching to touch his arm. "Rex, way too thoughtful."

She unwrapped them all, one by one, emotional as she held out what was inside. There was a year's membership to Totville, which ran baby and toddler classes. Ten children's books. A big stuffed penguin that was actually a baby chair. A fancy dress. A beaded bracelet that spelled out *Chloe*. Three teething toys. A savings bond.

"Um, I think this is way more than six gifts," she said, handing one of the teethers to Chloe, who shook it wildly with a big smile. "Rex, thank you. I love everything. And I know Chloe does, too. Don't you, sweetie?" She bent over to kiss the baby on her head.

Chloe shook the teething toy again, then chewed on it before looking at Rex and letting out a big laugh.

Maisey laughed, too. "That's her way of saying thank you."

"My pleasure, Chloe," Rex said, a little too aware of how special this baby was to him. "Merry Christmas."

This time it was Maisey who leaned forward and kissed him, hot on the lips. And not a fast kiss. Slow and sexy.

"Now we're even," she said.

"So we are," he said, unable to take his eyes off her, his gaze roaming around the curves of her red dress, her long legs, the supersexy black heels.

She popped up as if she needed a little escape from him and both kisses. "Well, time to get Chloe changed and ready for bed. I'll be back down in about fifteen minutes and then we can exchange gifts."

"I'll be here," he said, not wanting either of them to leave the room.

She looked at him, her expression shifting, and he could kick himself. *Here. But not for long.*

While she headed upstairs with Chloe, he picked up all the discarded wrapping paper and stuffed it into the empty bag. The doorbell rang, and the caterers wheeled away the cart.

He stared at the other shopping bag, the one with Maisey's gifts. He hoped he got it right.

Bringing the bag and his wine over to the sofa, which really was lumpy, he sat down and waited.

Finally, she was back, looking even sultrier somehow.

"I'm trying to look sexy, but these shoes are killing me," she said, kicking them off. "I almost tripped coming down the stairs, too."

"All about comfort," he said. "And you look just as sexy without the heels."

She wiggled her toes at him with a smile and sat down on the other end of the sofa. "Let me give you my present first, because if you went overboard for me, I won't feel as bad for only getting you one measly thing."

"What did you get me?" He couldn't even imagine what she'd choose for him.

She opened the drawer of the end table and pulled out a small wrapped box and handed it to him.

He ripped off the paper to find a gold box. Inside was a beautiful old bronze compass.

"It's antique," she said, "but I was assured it's as good as when it was brand-new. And the nice proprietor of the thrift shop engraved it for me. Turn it over and you'll see."

No matter where you are, I'll always be there for you.—Maisey.

Yes, he thought. *You will be. Because you* are *in my heart.*

"Follow your North Star and you'll always be on the right path," his grandfather used to say all the time. The US Marshals Service, finding fugitives, protecting witnesses—his North Star. His mission.

Except he didn't feel that in his heart, either. Which was unsettling. And maybe what had been bothering him lately. His commitment and dedication to his job was as strong as ever, but it was a head thing, not a heart thing. He'd felt the absence of it acutely when he realized his dad wasn't in there, either, after reading that letter. The letter that should have brought him peace and closure.

What the hell was up with him? *Sweep, sweep, sweep*, he told himself. *Stop thinking about it.* It was Christmas. He was here with Maisey.

He turned more fully toward her. "I love this, Maisey. More than I can even say. Thank you." He put it on the coffee table where he could see it instead of back in the box. Then he pulled over the other shopping bag with her gifts. "I did go kind of overboard, but that's just who I am."

He set out the gifts on the coffee table and watched her face light up every time she opened one. A plush white bathrobe and matching slippers. A gift certificate to the day spa in town, where she could get a massage. A red leather journal and a fancy pen to record all her hopes and dreams. A baby book to record milestones and include photos, which she pressed to her heart. Brochures for Western Wyoming University and their bachelor's in education. The last gift was the one he was a little worried about.

She ripped off the silver wrapping paper and opened the box. "Oh, Rex, it's so beautiful." It was an old-fashioned oval gold locket on a filigree chain.

"It opens," he said.

She clicked open the little latch. Inside was a recent picture of Chloe he'd taken the day he'd babysat her at the Kid Zone. He'd resized it to fit in the small locket.

She held it by the chain and examined all the facets. "I love it. I've never had anything like it. Will you do the honors?"

She faced away from him and moved her long blond hair to the side. He wanted to kiss her neck. He fastened the clasp, and she turned back around. "How does it look?" she asked, turning a bit and then right, her smile so beautiful.

"It looks perfect. Like you," he added on a whisper, unable to take his eyes off her face.

The next thing he knew, she was straddling him, her hands on his chest, her mouth fused to his.

He was losing the ability to reason, to even process that this was not only a bad idea but a potentially catastrophic one.

"I want tonight, Rex Dawson. I've taken back Christmas and I want this final night between us to be part of it. Tomorrow I'm sure you'll be with your family, and then the next day you're outta here. Tonight is about us."

Could he have this? He wanted it more than anything right now. But... "You're sure?"

If she even hesitated, he'd get up and take out their tiramisu from the refrigerator and suggest an action movie with lots of car chases.

"One hundred percent," she said and reached behind her to unzip her dress.

Chapter Fifteen

Maisey lay naked under the blanket in her bed, barely able to believe that Rex was equally naked beside her—fast asleep.

Wow. Wow, wow, wow.

She'd only been with one man. Now two. And wow.

He stirred beside her, turning his head slightly toward her, his eyes closed, the long dark eyelashes against his upper cheek. His hair was mussed from her hands inside it. He also might have a few scratches down his back, she thought, wanting to burst out of bed and do a little dance.

I love you, she told him silently.

His eyes opened slowly and lazily, and he pulled her to him, wrapping her in a hug. "Merry Christmas."

"Merry Christmas," she barely managed as warm gooey love spread through every part of her body, stealing her breath. "Last night was something, huh?"

He dropped a kiss on her shoulder. "Exceeded my wildest imaginings."

Her heart leaped. "So you imagined this? Us together in bed?" She'd hoped so and even figured as much, but Rex was a different breed of male and who really knew?

"All the time, Maisey."

She definitely liked knowing that. "I figured you were trying not to. To keep things platonic."

"Well, things should be platonic, but we both got caught up last night. The holiday. The wine..."

Her stomach dropped and her heart felt like a weight was pressing against it. She shifted away from him and lay back, staring at the ceiling. Oh, hell.

"So last night didn't change anything for you?" she asked, sitting up and looking right at him.

"It just made things harder," he said gently. "Harder to leave tomorrow morning." He turned away, clearly uncomfortable, then looked back at her. "Maisey, last night you said sex was about last night—only. Part of Christmas Eve, our last night together before I get wrapped up in family stuff, which of course I'd include you in, anyway."

"I know, but..." she said, the word choking on a sob that threatened to wrench out of her.

Yes, he was right. *You're sure?* he'd asked last night, waiting for her to respond. She'd said, *One hundred percent.* This was her fault. But she'd believed in the Christmas Eve, special gifts and wine haze that the sex, the intimacy, joining the two of them physically, would mean something to him. Something so powerful it would break through whatever was holding him back, keeping him from her, keeping him on the road.

"You're right," she said flatly. "I have no dibs on you."

"Maisey—"

She held up her hand. "Look, it's Christmas. I did want last night for exactly the reasons I said. And yes, I hoped that this morning you would suddenly turn into a different person."

One who loves me more than whatever has you so afraid of us.

"Not that I want you to be different, Rex. You're amazing. I just want you to *stay.*" She sucked in a breath. "I think I hear Chloe," she said and ran out of the room.

A little dramatic there, Maisey, she thought as

she rushed into the nursery and closed the door behind her. Chloe was fast asleep, not a peep out of her yet. But she'd needed space between them so she wouldn't burst into tears.

She stood by her daughter's crib, looking down at the baby sleeping in her festive holiday pj's. "Merry Christmas," she whispered.

A tap came at the door. She braced herself, then opened it. Rex was dressed, but barefoot, his hair less mussed.

"I—" he began.

"If you say you care deeply about me, I will throw this stuffed tiger at you," she said, picking it up from the bookcase by the door.

"I won't say it. But I do, Maisey. But I also need to leave tomorrow morning. I have a job and commitments. I've always been up-front about that."

You sure have. She could not be mad at him. She just wanted him to want her more, dammit.

"I used to want a family more than anything in the world, Rex. Now the only Christmas wish I have is for you to stay—with me. But that's not gonna happen. So go. But it's over between us, Rex. Don't text, don't call, don't come see me when you visit your family. It'll hurt too much. I have to accept that you don't love me. Because if you did, you wouldn't pick a lonely life on the road for a job that doesn't seem to suit you anymore. You wouldn't be able to *leave*. It's that simple."

"It's not, Maisey."

"Merry Christmas, Rex." *Let him go, let him go, let him go.*

Her heart clenched as he just stared at her, his blue eyes flashing with so much emotion she couldn't read. Finally, he nodded, then turned and headed toward the living room, where he'd left his socks and shoes. And the compass.

And then he was gone.

A few hours later, Rex sat on a flat rock by the river, way down from the guest cabins by at least five miles. If he walked north—and he had his antique compass to guide him—he'd eventually hit Axel's cabin, where he was expected for Christmas lunch in a little while. It was too cold to walk the half hour up there, so he was glad he'd driven, especially because he had bags of gifts in his SUV.

When he'd left Maisey's cabin earlier, he'd picked up River from Daisy's, thankful she wasn't home to interrogate him on why he looked so miserable, and he had no doubt he had and still did. He *felt* miserable. He and River had gone for a long walk in the woods up near Clover Mountain, the biting cold helping to clear his head. But then he'd think about how his sister had invited Maisey and Chloe to Christmas dinner tonight and how there was no way Maisey would show up after what had happened between them.

Which meant she'd be spending Christmas alone and hurt—and it was all his damned fault.

He shook his head and stared out at the water, watching the current rush over the rocks and big sticks. River was sniffing along the bank, on red alert for any signs of a chipmunk or squirrel. The fast-moving river reminded him how wild it was that Maisey's bottle had stayed put up by the leg of the footbridge in the nature preserve—as if waiting for him to find it.

He had his dog to thank for that. He watched the sweet shepherd mix tilting his head at a squirrel darting up a tree, his ears standing tall, his tail wagging.

Rex had screwed up terribly. His mission was to give Maisey a great Christmas so that he could go back to his life as a marshal, his head and heart settled as far as she was concerned, and he'd almost succeeded until things came to a head this morning.

He glanced at his phone to check the time— he had to head up to Axel's for lunch. "Ready, buddy?" he called to River, who came trotting over like the good boy he was. He knelt down beside the dog and buried his face in his soft fur, getting a lick on the neck. "I'm gonna miss you so hard."

His boss's face pushed into his mind—a good thing. Rex was expected at district headquarters in Cheyenne in the morning, and he'd resume the search for his witness. He'd be consumed by that, his mission, and that would help with the hole in his chest with what he was leaving behind.

As he drove up the gravel road to Axel's, he could see Noah and Sara walking up the porch steps with their twins in their carriers. Axel came out with Dude, Danny on his shoulders to welcome them, his nephew holding his ever-present caped stuffed lion. He pictured Chloe on his own shoulders a year from now, Maisey beside him, walking up these steps to visit, River trailing and sniffing behind them. If he were a different person, that person Maisey had once said she wished he was, he'd be living that life. He'd be a family man. But that wasn't who he was.

As he exited his SUV, he gave his head a little shake to clear it, then got distracted from the image since Dude came flying down the stairs to say hello to his bestie, River. Rex gave Dude a pat and went up the stairs behind the group, swallowed up in family festivities with no time to think—thank God.

They ate buffet-style in the family room and exchanged gifts, the kids scoring a major haul each since all the siblings had gone overboard, their MO. Rex got some great presents himself, from noise-canceling tiny earphones that would come in handy since he'd left his on a plane a few weeks ago, to a very soft cashmere sweater and scarf, to books, including one titled *Don't Let the One You Love Get Away.* Yup, that one was from Daisy, along with two pairs of Smartwool socks and a memory-foam neck pillow for his travels.

His very favorite gift was in his shirt pocket. The antique compass. He had no doubt he'd have it on him wherever he went. Maybe forever.

Daisy sat down beside him with a cup of eggnog. "So, I couldn't help but notice that you never came back last night, Rex. Mistletoe led to good things, I presume?" She stared at him, trying to read him, he knew, and narrowed her eyes, her mouth open. "Aha! You're blushing!"

His phone pinged. Saved by the text—*thank you, universe!*

"Sorry, important text," he told Daisy, holding up his phone sideways and dashing away into the hall, not that he had any idea who had sent it. He hoped it was Maisey, letting him know they could be friends eventually. That of course he could stop by to see her and Chloe when he visited his family at the ranch.

Which was unfair of him. How could they be friends after how they'd left things this morning? After he'd ruined her Christmas.

He eyed the screen and his eyes widened. The witness. Joseph Farmer.

Can you meet me right now? Same spot as last time? I promise to show up this time. I need to talk.

He texted back that he'd be there in twenty minutes, then glanced around the family room. His brothers were all playing with Danny, Tony and the twins watching from their baby swings. He hurried over to Daisy, who was biting into a snowman cookie with one hand and holding crumb-laden plates with the other on her way into the kitchen with Sadie. He called her over. "I have a work emergency," he whispered. "I have to go. Tell everyone I'm sorry. I might not be back to-night. I'm not sure. I'll stop by the farmhouse to quickly pack."

She nodded with a rueful smile. "You'll be back. But go do your thing." She looked at his empty hands. "Wait one tiny second." She flew over to the sofa and grabbed the big red bag with the gifts he'd received. "Just in case you don't get back tonight. But I know you will."

He took the bag and kissed her on the cheek and headed to the door, not realizing River had followed him until he turned to grab his jacket and scarf from the huge wrought-iron coatrack. The sight of the dog sitting in the hallway, staring at Rex with his tilted head, one ear straight up and the other sideways, just about broke him.

He knelt beside River. "I gotta go, buddy. If I can't come back tonight, I'll see you in a couple months. You take care of everyone, okay?" He gave him a hug and flew out the door, setting the bag on the floor of the back seat of his SUV.

Twenty minutes later, his duffel beside the bag of gifts he'd received, Rex reached the preserve and headed to the spot.

Where he'd found River. Where his heart had been stolen by a little girl's letter. Where the witness hadn't shown up. *Chasing ghosts...*

"Hey."

Rex whirled around, this time completely caught off guard, which wouldn't have happened two weeks ago. Or ever. He was distracted, his mind on other things. Home. His family. River.

Maisey. Chloe.

Joseph Farmer, the rogue witness who'd disappeared over two weeks ago, looked pale and worried. "I'm sorry for just disappearing on you. I want to explain. My ex-wife and I were pretty close to getting back together when my life fell completely apart because I saw that drug deal and could ID the kingpin."

"Oh, yeah?" Rex asked. He hadn't known anything about that. His office had been staking out the wife's condo a few towns away and there'd been no contact, as far as they knew. The Farmers had been divorced for almost two years, no kids. Both were in their early fifties.

Farmer nodded. "I've been talking to Val on a burner phone I sent her so that no one could track either side. Finally, today, a Christmas miracle. She said that we could have a second chance if I get all this behind me. That she'd go into witness protection with me. Is that possible?"

Rex nodded. "I'd put you in protective custody and then I'd make arrangements for her to join you." His boss would make it happen. Rex had no doubt.

The man's shoulders sagged with relief. "I thought if I disappeared into some new identity, I'd never get to hear her voice again, you know? We're not even married anymore because I was an idiot, but she never gave up on me. I want this second chance. That's all I care about."

Sometimes love—or the hope for it—really did

conquer all. He was especially grateful it worked for Joseph Farmer. Because it affected a lot of other people who needed him to testify. Including Rex.

"I'm happy for you, Mr. Farmer. Definitely a merry Christmas for you."

"And you, I bet. Sorry for everything I put you through."

"Part of the job," he said. *Chasing ghosts*, he thought again. His father had been right.

Anyway, you'll find this eventually, one day, and when you do, just know your father loved you, Rexy.

He put his hand to the left side of his chest, dimly aware of the faintest glimmer of Bo Dawson elbowing his way into Rex's heart. This past year, his father had forced Rex to take a long, long time to find what the key unlocked—so he'd be ready for it.

But what Maisey had taught him was that being ready was up to him.

"Let's go, then," Rex said. "A new life with your new love awaits."

The man pulled him into a bear hug and burst into tears, swiping under his eyes and sniffling. "I like how you put that. It is new. Well, old and new mixed together. Can't separate them." He glanced at Rex as they walked to his SUV. "You married?"

Rex shook his head. "Nah. Job means I live on the road."

Farmer grimaced. "The road is hell, Marshal. I've been on it for the past two weeks."

The compass Maisey gave him was in the inside pocket of his jacket. *No matter where you are, I'll always be there for you.—Maisey.*

He could definitely feel her in his chest, he thought, reaching up a hand to his heart again. She was there *with* him. She *was* his heart.

"I hear you on that," Rex said, opening the passenger door. Farmer got in and buckled up. By the time they were on the freeway, his witness, rogue no more, was fast asleep. Stress could do that to a person. As they arrived at the US Marshals Service district headquarters in Cheyenne, Joe was awake and less emotional, and even more resolute. He made a call on the burner phone to his ex, and she assured him she'd be right behind him for a *very* fresh start.

Since he was in Cheyenne, he headed to his condo. The place wasn't as sterile as he remembered, but there was nothing personal in it. It could be a hotel suite. He couldn't bear the thought of staying here, certainly not on Christmas, but he'd never make it back to Bear Ridge in time for the family dinner at Daisy's farmhouse. If he hurried, he could probably get there just in time for dessert. He could say a last goodbye to his family, to River.

To Maisey.

He pulled out the compass and turned toward north, thinking about his grandfather's words. *Follow your North Star and you'll always be on the right path.*

Maisey was his North Star. His passion. His reason for everything. There was no denying it anymore, though he'd clearly been trying since he'd met her. She'd eclipsed everything else.

He locked up and headed back to his car, noting he needed gas. A few filling stations were open. He pulled into one with a convenience store so he could grab a Coke and a pack of gum. His shoulder brushed a rack of sunglasses and Christmas paraphernalia, including ornaments, and he gently gripped the top of the rack to make sure it didn't topple over.

And that was when Rex froze, staring in disbelief at what was right in front of him. In this little store at a gas station off the service road was the Siamese cat ornament that Maisey had been holding when her father had rescued her from the house fire. The one that had been missing from her life since some cretin stole her Christmas tree from the trailer. Well, not the original, of course. But a replica.

He was sure it was the one. Siamese cat. Green eyes. Red-and-green bow tie. Long and skinny with an upturned tail. The picture he'd seen of it in her cabin was pressed to memory. This was definitely it.

"Half-off, by the way," the clerk called. "Not the sunglasses. Just the Christmas stuff."

The ornament was priceless.

He held it in his hand, and every moment of his relationship with Maisey Clark came flashing into his head. From the way he'd felt as he'd read her letter to Santa, meeting her for the first time at the Kid Zone, their work on the children's holiday show, Chloe in his arms as he sang her songs and showed her the reindeer out the lodge window. Maisey in her red dress.

Last night. Every beautiful bit of it.

He stared at the Siamese cat, a three-inch-tall painted wood ornament, and had to grip the display rack for a moment as a fierce realization hit him.

He *did* love Maisey. Loved her so much.

And he wasn't leaving until he hung this ornament on the tree in her cabin. It was a way to save her Christmas, maybe, let her know how much he did care.

If she'd even let him in.

Chapter Sixteen

Maisey stared out the window of her cabin at the lightly falling snow. Instead of marveling over the white Christmas, she just wanted to scream *Bah humbug!* at the top of her lungs. But then she'd wake up Chloe, whom she'd put down for the night only a half hour ago.

Maisey had felt even worse about having to miss dinner at Daisy's, but she couldn't exactly have texted Rex not to show up so that she could go. So she'd texted Daisy that she wasn't feeling well, which was true, and Daisy had texted back that she'd send over a plate—of course she would—and that the family would miss her and

Rex. Daisy had clearly thought Maisey knew Rex had left during lunch because she'd added a few details about that and Maisey had pieced together that he'd gotten a call from work to come in.

She squeezed her eyes shut as pain gripped her. Rex was already gone.

You knew what would happen, she told herself. *And you let it happen because it had to— speeding train and all that, because who could stop a speeding train?*

She reached for the locket around her neck. What was she supposed to do with this? If she wore it, she'd be reminded of Rex. Like now. The locket symbolized everything between them, but the truth was, there wasn't anything. Not anymore.

He gave you back Christmas. He gave you the knowledge that you can fall in love. That great men are out there. He enriched your life. And now he's gone and you have to accept it.

Tonight, though, because it was Christmas, she'd wallow. She had a pint of Ben & Jerry's Cherry Garcia and she'd watch *When Harry Met Sally* or *Bridget Jones's Diary* and then she'd fall asleep and it wouldn't be Christmas and her new routine would start. Her life without Rex.

The doorbell rang and she dragged herself over, expecting to find Daisy's husband or another Dawson with the plate of traditional Christmas dinner Daisy had said she'd send over.

But it was Rex standing on the doorstep.

"You're far away, though," she said. "Daisy told me you were called in to work."

"I was. I had to take care of something important, but it's done now." Right on the doorstep, the cold night air and snowflakes around them, he told her about the witness and his ex-wife and how they were going to have a second chance in the witness protection program.

"Well, that worked out," she said. "It almost sounds romantic, though I'm sure it'll be a tough adjustment. But they'll do it together."

Why was she standing there talking about another couple?

"I have something for you, Maisey," he said, and she noticed the small white bag in his hand.

He reached inside and held up the ornament she'd been looking for for so many years. She covered her mouth with her hands and burst into tears.

"Can I come in, Maisey?"

She shook her head. "No. No, you can't."

"I was in a gas station convenience store in Cheyenne, and there it was, on a rack of half-price Christmas stuff. It's a Christmas miracle, huh."

He held out the Siamese cat ornament. "You don't have to allow me in. But please accept it, Maisey."

She sniffled and took the ornament and went over to the tree, looking for just the spot for it. She took off a red ball that was front and center and hung the cat ornament on the branch, dimly aware that Rex had come inside and shut the door.

"Thank you for bringing it, Rex. For finding it. You're good at that." She tried for a smile but her tears welled harder. Dammit.

Snowbell brushed along his ankles and he picked up the cat and gave her a nuzzle, getting white hairs on his black leather jacket.

"You'd better go now," she said. "I'm happy to have the ornament, I really am, but my heart is broken, Rex. It's my own stupid fault and—"

He stepped up close and took her hands. "No. It's not your fault. You're optimistic and open and loving, Maisey Clark. It's my fault. But maybe I can fix things."

"Rex, we had this conversation. I can't—"

"Finding that ornament—sheer dumb luck by picking one gas station over another—blew me away, Maisey. And knocked some truths into my head that I can't ignore anymore."

"Like what?" she asked.

"Like that I love you more than anything else in the world. I love Chloe. I thought I didn't want to be a dad until that baby girl grabbed hold of my heart. I love you. And if you'll still have me, I'm not going anywhere. I'm staying."

She wrapped her arms around him. "Oh, I'll have you. I love you, too. Obviously."

He grinned and hugged her tight and kissed her, then stepped back to look at her. "Will you marry me, Maisey?"

She gasped, tears running down her cheeks. She tried to find the word *yes* but couldn't speak.

"The gas station had some gumball machines, and there was one that sold big very faux diamond rings for fifty cents, but I'd rather wait till the jewelry shop in Prairie City opens tomorrow. I want you to have the engagement ring of your dreams. Not that you said yes."

She grinned. "Yes, Rex. A million times yes. And a charm machine ring would have been just fine." She flew into his arms, holding him tight. "Just like you to make every one of my Christmas dreams come true."

"I didn't even know I had Christmas dreams until I met you, Maisey. I—"

The doorbell interrupted him, and she opened the door to find his brother Ford standing there holding a huge plate.

"Merry Christmas," he said. "Daisy sent me with traditional Christmas dinner. We all hope you feel better." He peered around her. "Rex? You're not here. You're off chasing justice."

Rex laughed. "I was but I'm back. In every sense of the word. I'll be talking to the chief about that other opening at the Bear Ridge PD. Looks like we're gonna be colleagues."

Ford extended his hand. "Glad to hear it. I get to make Daisy's night."

"Well, tell her it gets even better. She's about to get a new sister-in-law. Maisey and I are engaged."

Ford's eyes lit up, and he hugged Maisey, then Rex. "Welcome to the family, Maisey."

She grinned. He had no idea what those words meant to her.

After Ford left, Rex took the plate and eyed it. "I missed Christmas dinner and this looks amazing. Turkey, stuffing, ham, mashed potatoes, Daisy's awful green-bean casserole—don't tell her I said that."

Maisey laughed. "I'm starving, too. We get to have Christmas dinner together after all."

"For many decades to come," he said. "I'm going to be a father," he added, his eyes glistening.

"Chloe's very lucky and so am I."

"We'll have a house built here or in town. Whatever you want, Maisey."

"I'd love to live on the ranch. I don't need anything fancy. Just you and Chloe and Snowbell and River. I almost forgot that I get a dog!"

He put down the plate on the kitchen table and pulled her into a hug, the snow swirling around outside the window, the multicolored lights of the evergreen twinkling. "Merry Christmas, Maisey."

"Merry Christmas," she whispered. "I can't wait to be Maisey Clark Dawson."

He smiled. "And how does Chloe Dawson sound? I'd love to adopt her. And if you'd like to look into adopting a child from foster care, I'm with you all the way. We can have five kids if you want. Six, maybe."

She held her fiancé tight, thinking of that little girl who wrote a letter to Santa, stuffed it in a bottle and tossed it in the creek that fed into the Bear Ridge River, hoping it would be found, that her Christmas wish would come true.

Fifteen years later, it did—and then some.

* * * * *

*Don't miss the next book in the
Dawson Family Ranch series,*
Wyoming Cinderella,
*coming in February 2021
from Harlequin Special Edition!*

*And in the meantime, check out these
other great single-mom romances:*

The Single Mom's Second Chance
by Kathy Douglass

The Matchmaker's Challenge
by Teresa Southwick

The Sheriff's Star
by Makenna Lee

*Available now wherever Harlequin Special
Edition books and ebooks are sold!*

WE HOPE YOU ENJOYED
THIS BOOK FROM

SPECIAL
EDITION

Believe in love. Overcome obstacles. Find happiness.

Relate to finding comfort and strength in the
support of loved ones and enjoy the journey
no matter what life throws your way.

6 NEW BOOKS AVAILABLE EVERY MONTH!

COMING NEXT MONTH FROM

♦ HARLEQUIN
SPECIAL EDITION

Available December 1, 2020

#2803 A COWBOY'S CHRISTMAS CAROL
Montana Mavericks: What Happened to Beatrix?
by Brenda Harlen

Evan Cruise is haunted by his past and refuses to celebrate the festivities around him—until he meets Daphne Taylor. But when Daphne uncovers Evan's shocking family secret, it threatens to tear them apart. Will a little Christmas magic change everything?

#2804 A TEMPORARY CHRISTMAS ARRANGEMENT
The Bravos of Valentine Bay • by Christine Rimmer

Neither Harper Bravo nor Lincoln Stryker is planning to stay in Valentine Bay. But when Lincoln moves in next door and needs a hand with his nice and nephew, cash-strapped Harper can't help but step in. They make a deal: just during the holiday season, she'll nanny the kids while he works. But will love be enough to have them both changing their plans?

#2805 HIS LAST-CHANCE CHRISTMAS FAMILY
Welcome to Starlight • by Michelle Major

Brynn Hale has finally returned home to Starlight. She's ready for a fresh start for her son, and what better time for it than Christmas? Still, Nick Dunlap is the one connection to her past she can't let go of. Nick's not sure he deserves a chance with her now, but the magic of the season might make forgiveness—and love—a little bit easier for them both...

#2806 FOR THIS CHRISTMAS ONLY
Masterson, Texas • by Caro Carson

A chance encounter at the town's Yule log lighting leads Eli Taylor to invite Mallory Ames to stay with him. Which turns into asking her to be his fake girlfriend to show his siblings what a genuinely loving partnership looks like...just while they visit for the holidays. But will their lesson turn into something real for both of them?

#2807 A FIREHOUSE CHRISTMAS BABY
Lovestruck, Vermont • by Teri Wilson

After her dreams of motherhood were dashed, Felicity Hart is determined to make a fresh start in Lovestruck. Unfortunately, she has to work with firefighter Wade Ericson when a baby is abandoned at the firehouse. Then Felicity finds herself moving into Wade's house and using her foster-care training to care for the child, all just in time for Christmas.

#2808 A SOLDIER UNDER HER TREE
Sweet Briar Sweethearts • by Kathy Douglass

When her ex-fiancé shows up at her shop—engaged to her sister!—dress designer Hannah Carpenter doesn't know what to do. Especially when former fling Russell Danielson rides to the rescue, offering a fake relationship to foil her rude relations. The thing is, there's nothing fake about his kiss...

**YOU CAN FIND MORE INFORMATION ON UPCOMING HARLEQUIN TITLES,
FREE EXCERPTS AND MORE AT HARLEQUIN.COM.**

HSECNM1120

*Brynn Hale, single mom widowed after an unhappy
marriage, has finally returned home to Starlight.
She's ready for a fresh start for her son, and what
better time for it than Christmas? But Nick Dunlap is
the one connection to her past she can't let go of...*

*Read on for a sneak peek at the next book in the
Welcome to Starlight miniseries,*
His Last-Chance Christmas Family
by Michelle Major.

"You sound like a counselor." The barest glimmer of
a smile played around the edges of Brynn's mouth.
"When did you get so smart, Chief Dunlap?"

"I was born this way. You never noticed before now
because you were too dazzled by my good looks."

Her eyes went wide for a moment, and he wondered
if he'd overstepped with the teasing. "I was dazzled
by you. That part is true." She rolled her eyes. "But I
guarantee you didn't show this kind of insight when we
were younger."

He should make some funny comment back to her,
keep the moment light. Instead, he let his gaze lower to
her mouth as he took the soft ends of her hair between

his fingers. "I might not have messed things up so badly if I had."

She drew in a sharp breath and he stepped away. This was not the time to spook her. "Come on, Brynn," he coaxed. "We both know it's not going to be good for anyone if you stay with your mom."

"She doesn't even want to meet Remi," Brynn told him, her full lips pressing into a thin line.

"Her loss," he said quietly. "All along it's been her loss. Say yes. Please."

She shifted and looked to where Tyler had disappeared with Kel. Without turning back to Nick, she nodded. "Yes," she said finally. "Thank you for the offer. I appreciate it and promise we won't disrupt your life." Now she did turn to him. "Very much, anyway," she added with a smile.

"Easy as pie," he said, ignoring the fact that his heart was beating as fast as if he'd just finished running a marathon.

Don't miss
His Last-Chance Christmas Family *by Michelle Major,*
available December 2020 wherever
Harlequin Special Edition books and ebooks are sold.

Harlequin.com

Get 4 FREE REWARDS!

We'll send you 2 FREE Books plus 2 FREE Mystery Gifts.

Harlequin Special Edition books relate to finding comfort and strength in the support of loved ones and enjoying the journey no matter what life throws your way.

FREE
Value Over
$20

YES! Please send me 2 FREE Harlequin Special Edition novels and my 2 FREE gifts (gifts are worth about $10 retail). After receiving them, if I don't wish to receive any more books, I can return the shipping statement marked "cancel." If I don't cancel, I will receive 6 brand-new novels every month and be billed just $4.99 per book in the U.S. or $5.74 per book in Canada. That's a savings of at least 12% off the cover price! It's quite a bargain! Shipping and handling is just 50¢ per book in the U.S. and $1.25 per book in Canada.* I understand that accepting the 2 free books and gifts places me under no obligation to buy anything. I can always return a shipment and cancel at any time. The free books and gifts are mine to keep no matter what I decide.

235/335 HDN GNMP

Name (please print)

Address   Apt. #

City   State/Province   Zip/Postal Code

Email: Please check this box ☐ if you would like to receive newsletters and promotional emails from Harlequin Enterprises ULC and its affiliates. You can unsubscribe anytime.

Mail to the **Reader Service:**
IN U.S.A.: P.O. Box 1341, Buffalo, NY 14240-8531
IN CANADA: P.O. Box 603, Fort Erie, Ontario L2A 5X3

Want to try 2 free books from another series! Call 1-800-873-8635 or visit www.ReaderService.com.